RANGER'S DILEMMA

TEXAN DEVILS

SOFIA AVES

A TEXAN DEVILS NOVELLA

SOFIA AVES

First Edition

Published by Little Quail Press

ISBN EBOOK978-1-922448-68-2

ISBN PRINT 978-1-923471-22-1

Previously published in part in the *One Last Kiss* charity anthology.

for all who love with a full heart

CHAPTER ONE

COLE

I straightened my shoulders for the fiftieth time in an hour, threw on a winning smile I was growing to hate, and mangled my line.

Again.

"Texas Rangers deal with a higher level of criminal on a daily basis who—"

"No!" A stout, round man dressed in a black vest over tweed pants and a black beret approached me, looking for all the world something out of a horror film, or a reality TV show. Which was pretty much what this documentary farce was fast coming to be.

He raised his hand and waved frantically, even though silence had already fallen all around the small crew gathered in the Texas field far from any road or other part of civilization that I recognized.

"I need you standing here. Yes. No, no, no. Yes. In the spotlight, please sir."

The Director with a capital D that stood for something a lot less kind in my personal narrative–though that thankfully never made it to my mouth–manhandled me about in an awkward as fuck two-step until I was sick of all physical contact with another human being.

When he was finally happy with poking and prodding me, I ended up standing in the same spot I started, and facing the same way.

I gritted my teeth and counted backwards from twenty, running through memories of the worst call outs I attended as a Texas cop, and my remaining jobs left during my first week as a Texas Ranger on Rhys Archer's team. It didn't take a genius to realize that with the documentary crew in town for the duration of their filming season, I had no chance in hell of getting anything done, which included starting my new job.

I stared over Director D's head and caught the eye of a pretty blonde girl clutching a clipboard. Dark glasses framed her heart shaped face, giving her a pre-Harley Quinn-esque sort of look, all long hair, high cheekbones, and intelligent eyes.

Soft lips formed a natural pout that fell in a pretty rose bud bow. I swallowed back a sharp wave of an insta-lust, and blamed it on the pure boredom of filming from daybreak 'til sundown. So far my daily achievements included uttering the grand total of eighteen words for the day on repeat like a well-trained parrot, and no break for lunch in sight. I stared at the darkening horizon.

Or dinner.

The girl shifted, drawing my attention away from what I was supposed to be doing and back to her. She watched everything around her through bright eyes that her Clark Kent style glasses couldn't disguise, and scratched something out on her clip-board. A grin tugged at the corners of my lips as I watched her work. That woman should be the person running the show while Director Dandy pants pranced about like a semi-functioning unicorn in a babyshit brown suit even an accountant wouldn't dare wear.

Josie Petersen. I'd seen her running around the impromptu set, helping everyone in sight for even the most trivial issues–including the dreaded coffee run from the thermos table since we were bang in the middle of bumfuck nowhere–and my respect for her grew. More than once her comments had been incredibly insightful and far more useful than the D-words's pomp and pandering.

Someone save me, I mouthed, barely moved my lips. If I stood still any longer I might as well have *marionette* tattooed on my forehead with Director D-bag holding the strings. The girl caught my eye, watching me as a pretty-in-pink stain spread across her cheeks. She pursed her lips thoughtfully. I instantly wanted to kiss her for the hell of it, indulging in my mini daydream fantasy.

Director D stepped back, cutting his hands across my field of vision. "Bellissimo!'

Bellissimo? Who the fuck says Bellissimo?

"You might be new to our world, but I believe you have the sparkle of a star. Just like that. Stay right there. Smile! And *do not move*."

"I fucking hate this show." I spoke to my teeth softly enough for the cameraman at my back to hear, but fortunately the director missed my excess of snark.

"And, action...!"

It was like the man expected me to do something after telling me to stand still, say nothing, and *do* nothing except pose.

The opposite of everything I trained myself to be.

"Well?" The little man stood in front of me with his hands pressed to his pudgy hips. His gaze slipped sideways, and his hands shifted to his middle, rolling over each other in the universal *get going* motion. "Do something," he hissed.

"Oh."

Eloquent, Cole. Real fucking eloquent. You're painting the Rangers in a brilliant light.

Archer told me about the doco on my first day in his office. As a transfer from one of the border Texas Rangers units focused on preventing narcotics entering the US, and people trafficking, I was used to dealing with Brodie in his undercover capacities and infiltrations inside the cartels.

What I wasn't used to was being thrown into the spotlight, doing little except standing around.

Brodie spoke highly of Archer and his unit, and I knew he'd done the same for me in reference. I had a feeling that despite the hours I put into working with the Ranger's in the borderlands and my career as a Texas law enforcement officer previously that the stocky Ranger's recommendation was what got me where I stood today.

In the spotlight, posing like a bodybuilder on stage with all the gym-based muscles and nothing of true value to offer than looking pretty. I'd essentially become a showgirl. The double standards placed on the film industry and genders in all their variation never hit me so damn hard. Perspective was great but right now I could do with a little less on the front line.

Maybe I could pull an upside from the experience after all, and draw on a little more empathy in my day to day dealings. A tenuous grasp on the positive, but I'd take it. Anything to feel *useful* after standing around all day. Hell, my feet even hurt for all the wrong reasons.

Archer threw me in the deep end with his trademark grin and informed me that if I didn't show up the Rangers in the best light possible I'd find myself back on the border force with little chance of seeing my Austin based apartment for a very long time.

Maybe around the time he retired.

Director D-bag gave me the feeling the small man would take delight in ruining the Austin based Texas Ranger elite unit's reputation Archer worked so hard to preserve. Even I knew there was no coming back from a marked record career wise, I got the impression that Archer's gut was absolutely correct.

My respect for the man grew even as he shunted me out of his office door with a brief pat on the shoulder and an easy, '*Good luck, son.*'

Son? I was old enough to be his brother, his twin brother, for fuck's sake. Both of us were a year shy of the big four-oh. But he didn't know me, and I didn't know him, though I'd heard the rumors. We all had. Archer handpicked the best investigators the Rangers have seen in years, with his photo in color framed in the portrait gallery wall at HQ while he was still alive, no less. That was a blaring tribute in itself. If only there was a bar with his name on it and not belatedly after the fact, then he would know he'd really made it.

The sun dipped below the horizon, leaving the scene in a field of purple haze that shadowed every face around me. Heat disappeared with the last of the sunlight, replaced by the sinking chill of a cold night to come.

"Unbelievable." The director waved at me as I stared off into the distance. "And that's it for the day."

I winced, coming back to myself. The crew had

already started packing up their gear. Josie peered over her clipboard, offering a shy smile and a mini thumbs up near her cheeks. I grinned back. It was good to have an ally when I'd been thrown into a brand new arena and had no damn idea what I was doing, let alone possibly compete effectively there.

The Director's words filtered past my distraction and flirting as the movement around me clicked in.

"But I didn't do anything." My protest died as the Director moved off, waving his hand in dismissal while I was left addressing a guy still clutching his camera offering micro-expressions of desperation.

"Oh, we all know Texas Rangers never do anything important. It's all pose here, and stare out there, all to keep those on the other side of the law in line, right?" His disparaging comments undermined twenty years of law enforcement bred into my veins in an instant.

This is going to be a fucking long season.

At Archer's behest I signed up for at least eight episodes, maybe twelve. It looked like the first one just wrapped up and I barely said a word. Which meant there was a whole lot of space for Director D to fill with his happy little misconceptions.

If all the doco crew were going to do was use me as a poster boy, I wouldn't be able to hold up the end of the bargain I'd shaken hands on with Archer, and

I wouldn't be invited back to his unit again. Apart from career death, the part that really bugged me was the decent dose of pride I took in being part of the Texas Rangers. D-bag's attitude bothered me at a deep, personal level. The Rangers were the top of the food chain in the Texas law enforcement world, and I wanted to make sure that we lived up to the legend, rather than be poorly portrayed as the muscle bound warrior in a white hat, staring off into the distance.

The camera crew cleared up around me in complete silence, and I was left standing in the middle of nowhere, doing nothing, holding my literal hat in my hands.

I tried not to fidget and had no idea what to do with myself. It was like being back in kindergarten all over again. "Jesus fucking Christ."

Tomorrow would be a better day. I promised myself I wouldn't let a repeat performance of day one's farce happen again.

"I thought you did well," a soft voice murmured behind me. "For a first timer."

I swiveled on my heel to face the Harley Quinn girl. *Josie.* I begged her name off one of the camera monkeys early on, and was glad to see I wasn't the only one wearing a glazed expression when she walked by.

"Thanks, but I doubt I did my career justice." *Or the unit.* I wasn't sure which irked me more, but they both reeked of pride and ego, something I'd opted to avoid in my Ranger career.

She shrugged. "Nobody does with Rennie. He's infamous for creating a scandal out of nothing and putting people down. Sorry." She winced while I remained stoic, lest I trip on my tongue to add to the kerfuffle of the day. "You really are very new to this aren't you?"

"Film virgin in a whorehouse." It was my turn to wince. "I'm sorry, ma'am. It's been a long day." Starting just before sunrise to be primped and puffed, I'd never felt more like a show dog in my life for the amount of makeup that had been plastered to my face. "I usually have better manners."

"I know." She continued to watch me beneath her lashes while managing to scribble something on her clipboard. I didn't know she utilized both skills at once. "I'm Josie."

I know. But I didn't want to own up to my little stalker moment just yet.

"Hi, Josie. You don't happen to have an hour for a Ranger to get dinner and a drink, do you?" I smiled, in what I hoped was a nice way, but her long, arched lashes widened a fraction, and I realized what I just said.

A snicker from the remaining crew taking their leave for the night backed that assumption up a hundredfold.

My hand rose to rub at the back of my neck on autopilot. I was well out of practice in either the dating pool or the social one, and I wanted to be in neither. This Ranger might have posed all day, but during any other week I barely had time to find my own bed, often sleeping at the office when I wasn't undercover, and getting up with the sun to do it all over again.

Qualities I was certain were undesirable in a dating partner, even if I was out of touch.

I sucked in a short, hard breath and tried again. "That's..." I rephrased my words ten times in quick succession and gave it up as a bad job. *Awkward much, Cole?* "Do you have time to educate a man who is so far out at his depth that he needs a pair of floaties and a bubble device to bring him back?"

"I do." She smiled brightly at me. "And I hear there's a new little sushi place opened up. I mean, it's all new to me, because I'm new to this town and I know where nothing is but apparently it's good. I don't know if you've been there? I mean, you might have been."

She closed her mouth and bit both lips at once. Her eyes flared in alarm, pink stealing in to color her cheeks. Rather than annoying, I found her easy chatter endearing, and could easily have listened to her and watched her cheeks turn red all evening.

I smiled, dropping a shoulder in a learned position to put her at ease. "I'd love that."

After a shitty day on a coerced job I'd managed to have part of a decent conversation with a pretty girl. That had to count for something. Josie stopped biting her lips, letting them plump out all pink and puffy to match her cheeks. My heart thumped a little harder as the tip of her tongue flicked out to swipe at a drop of moisture left there.

I swallowed, and tried to turn away from her, but couldn't. *Distraction achieved.* I cleared my throat and tried not to let my mind slip to other parts of her body that might flush pink or slick her skin with moisture.

The hell is wrong with me?

I ask a girl out of a platonic dinner date for *company*, for fuck's sake, and here I was, standing in the middle of a field, brutally eye fucking the poor girl. I wouldn't have blinked if she'd run all the way to where our vehicles were parked.

But Josie didn't run. She took a hesitant step toward me, one hand half-raised in my direction. "Cole?"

Now, if only I could have an investigation to

work on or something that actually used brain cells and gray matter.

That wasn't as far away as I expected. I smiled back but Josie looked past my shoulder, her mouth falling open in a pretty 'o' shape that sent every drop of blood in my body rushing south.

"Oh, my God."

I spun on my heel enough to almost fall on my ass, but it was her neck that cracked as she pushed past me in a flurry of soft hands and delayed response.

A young twenty-something man I recalled from the camera crew lay on the ground a dozen meters behind me, twitching as though he was in the middle of a fit. Josie's slow, dream-like steps sped up until she sprinted the short distance and fell to her knees.

"Call the ambulance," I called as I followed her. "We're on Burnham Road. The nearest corner is Hatchley St."

I pointed at the nearest stage crew personnel, though plenty came running at the commotion. A ridiculously bright bulb illuminated the area, flaring over the area. Someone had the nous to turn on a giant spotlight, likely saved for emergency night scenes...and not the sort we currently attended.

I reached Josie as she stretched her hands out as

though seeking to help the boy, but he let out a gurgle and she pulled them back sharply to cover her own mouth. A muffled cry broke from her as I gently shifted her aside to reach the kid.

Dormant skills that could have curled up and died over boredom for the day burst to life in a shot of pure adrenaline. My hands moved of their own accord, already taking in the way the kid's mouth clenched as his body shook, pushing the encroaching crowd back while keeping an eye on him, but thankfully there was nothing for him to hurt himself on.

I wracked my brain, trying to think through the process long buried beneath undercover stints and narcotics and trauma recovery information. It had been a long damn time since I helped anyone suffering a seizure. Jesus Christ, I needed to update my first aid course. That was top of my list tonight, as soon as this was done. But that didn't help me right now. Beside me, the kid trembled on the ground, his eyes glazed and bugged, unseeing.

Behind me, someone shouted the directions I gave earlier, and a wave of relief swept through me. At least there was enough reception to get a call out.

Slowly, the young man's tremors subsided. I memorized his features: early twenties, maybe twenty-five with good genes. No early lines on his face, a thick mop of sandy brown hair covering his face. Brown eyes. Nothing to distinguish him from any other human really. Average height, though he currently curled into a ball on his side, panting as the seizure released its grasp on him.

His chest rose and fell, and for a moment I had the dumbass clarity of thought to think we were good. I breathed out my relief only to choke on it as a small amount of foam spewed past his lips. The bubbles turned pink in the next instant, and nails clawed into my arm through my shirt.

Josie leaned forward, hovering beside me as I tried to help the kid who looked like he was O'Ding in front of me. But her whispered words were what froze me on the spot.

"Oh, hell. Not again."

CHAPTER TWO

JOSIE

Mister Texas Poser stepped into the situation like he'd found the thing he was meant to do, because it sure as shit wasn't standing in front of a camera. Cole Vance hadn't fit anywhere all day. That much was obvious in the way he stood, trying not to jitter or shove his hands in his pockets too many times, while his gaze fixed on a set point beyond the lights like he could wish his way back to whatever it was he did day to day.

There's nothing quite like watching a man who knows action but doesn't have it.

Director Rennie was infamous for taking someone amazing and turning them into crap on screen, ruining lives and careers without a care, providing he got his ratings and thus earned his astronomical paycheck. My summer intern job post college and before the real career was meant to start turned into a nightmare when I realized what he was like, but by then I signed my contract and it was too late to back out.

Cole Vance was nothing like the Director who spent his day trying to punch holes in the veteran Ranger's resolve. Watching Cole turn the younger man onto his side to try to clear his airway while shooing off anyone who stepped inside an invisible line he drew around his ward was magical. Not in the Hollywood-esque sense, but as though he were the predator protecting his kill.

Except it wasn't his prey. This man saved lives, rather than taking them.

And there was the broken romantic in me who wanted to make happy films, not the emotional chaos that Rennie created, ripping an honest man apart until he was left with nothing more than his worst deeds in office while the assholic director walked away unscathed and typically bored.

I didn't want to see that happen to this Texas Ranger.

The chattering crowd hushed as an ambulance pulled into the field up on the road, its singular lights against a deep purple backdrop a reminder of how far away we were from the main road, or anywhere. I clung to Cole's wrist, looking behind us. Austin's glow made a semi halo at the horizon to our east against the darkening sky. The hard lighting lit the field around us but ruined any chance of encouraging night vision outside our little spotlight. Beyond that, it might as well have been midnight.

"You're going to be okay, bud. No stress. Get you a decent doc and a cute nurse. Like nurses, man? I'll find you the prettiest one in Austin if you can manage a deep breath..."

I started to object to Cole's smooth murmur, his voice rolling like dark chocolate around us, but it took me less than a second to realize he didn't expect a response. The man in front of me transformed from the makeup-clad Texas Ranger into a really tall cop in a white hat, talking a person through trauma like he did this every day.

At some point in his career, he probably had.

Something warm uncoiled in my chest as I knelt and pressed a hand to Cole's shoulder. I didn't know if he registered the contact, but I knew those signs, and I'd grown up with a father who did the same thing every time I hurt myself. Sometimes it was overkill, but most of the time I appreciated the gesture.

Mostly.

Cole reminded me of the man my father used to be.

I shifted into a crouch, my thighs already screaming. After a minute with no change to the crewman I tried to straighten but Cole's hand wrapped around mine and squeezed tight. A tingle shot through my fingers and up my arm at the contact, but right now wasn't the time to analyze the reaction to his skin on mine.

Settling back beside him, our fingers tangled together, I watched the Texas Ranger in full swing. His strong, firm movement spoke of his capacity to work under pressure and his ability to focus in a crisis. Paul stopped bubbling, his breaths softening as his terror eased, his eyes closed. Some of the panic that reduced my chest capacity loosened.

"Thank God." Cole let his head hang, squeezing my hand tighter.

Around us, the crew muttered, and though I couldn't make out the words, I knew what they were saying. It was the same thing that shifted in my head the moment I saw those pink bubbles. But Paul, he seemed to be breathing better now, though I knew he was far from being out of danger.

Cole released my hand to grip Paul's. My skin grew cold at the lack of contact, though it only lasted an instant. He kept on talking as the ambulance pulled up to the edge of the scene, and two paramedics jumped out. He managed to stay out of their way but help at the same time, lifting as needed, still talking in that low, soothing voice that could have lulled me to sleep any night of the week.

David, one of the crew members, held a portable camera on his shoulder, the top red light glowing as it recorded. I hoped Cole didn't see as I got the impression he hated the whole charade of filming. I motioned him to back up and he flipped me the bird, though he did take a few steps back.

Discreet.

I rolled my eyes and turned my attention back to the scene at hand.

"Not bad, huh?" Owen, one of Rennie's full time writers, leaned in to whisper in my ear, ignoring the fact that Cole was right beside us. "It's like he was born for this shit. Not like the crap we had to watch all day."

"Something like that," I murmured.

Though I didn't agree with Owen's full sentiment, I knew what he meant. Clutching my clipboard to my chest, I nodded, and cast a quick glance around for the director who seemed to hear everything, but for once Rennie was nowhere in sight.

Cole caught the motion; his body tensed and he reacted in a totally different way as soon as I let my hand slip from his.

Not that we kept secrets, but being his first day, I wasn't sure how many rumors he'd been subject to, and which he'd chosen to believe or not, just yet. Or maybe he hadn't heard me, and reacted to the situation instead. Something in the way he touched me, moving me to one side, told me I had it right the first time.

I rose on slightly unsteady legs, backing up as a paramedic approached, already chatting with Cole as she checked over Paul's prone form.

"Gonna go out with him?" Owen squeezed my shoulder, his voice leering at me even if I couldn't see his face. "Looks like he might move fast from what he said...before," he grinned slyly.

I winced at the unwanted physical contact. "Cole wants company, not romance. It's pretty obvious he felt out of place all day, if you ask me. And right now...I think we should focus on Paul, don't you?" It came out preachier than I meant, but he asked after all.

That Cole actually had asked me on a date sat all too well in my stomach. The idea itself sent a shiver over me but the Texas Ranger straightened, rubbing a hand over his defined jaw in an unintentional but sexy as hell movement that drew my eye.

Tall, broad shouldered with a head of soft brown, almost blond hair, a strong jaw and white teeth, Cole Vance was the epitome of a typical western poster boy. If he didn't wear a white hat, I swore the Wild West would come door knocking for him. He filled out his shirt in all the right places, leaving me to imagine the hard muscle hiding beneath, and he wore that white hat just fine.

No wonder he was the man they'd sent out to film for the doco, but something with him all day hadn't felt right, like he hadn't wanted to be there. Or maybe it was just standing around all day. After seeing him in action for the last minute, I could understand what the last twelve hours felt like to him—long and wasteful.

Cole sent me a rueful glance, though his stance shifted, that sexy jawline–who thought of a *jawline* as sexy?–hardening as he spotted Rennie's assistant standing slightly behind me like an unwanted shadow.

"I think he wants a bit more than to feel all *included*," Owen grated in my ear.

I stepped forward, away from Rennie's leech, and closer to Cole without a word. Torn between being tempted to rip Owen a new one, not allowing my snark to screw my career on the spot, and letting out a banshee yell of epic proportions at the top of my lungs to voice my frustrations, I settled on a huff that could be interpreted one of a dozen ways.

Not that it should matter at all when a man was being carried away to an ambulance in front of me. Screaming in situ would be considered poor form, at best.

"Hey, Josie." Cole twisted on the spot as the paramedic he'd spoken to moved off with Paul on the stretcher. "Give me a few minutes to file a report, ask a few questions, huh? I'd love to try that sushi place with you." His disarming grin did odd things to my stomach.

Owen walked away behind me, his low, mocking laugh echoing in the open space, but I ignored him even when Cole's eyes flicked away from me for a second, following the other man's retreat.

"Sure. I'll help....pack up. Or something." I glanced around the area but most of the gear was already packed away as people broke off and headed for their own rental cars and temporary accommodation. "Rennie," I called, trotting to the director's side. "Can I help set up anything for tomorrow? Are you heading to the hospital with Paul?" I asked in a too-bright voice but no one was around to hear my insecurity, and Rennie wasn't likely to notice anyone's concerns but his own.

"Jodie, Josie," Rennie corrected himself in a sing-song voice totally inappropriate for the situation. He swiped an arm across his mouth and sniffed hard. "Yes, sure you can go to the hospital. I need to edit today's film and things…" His eyes glazed under the tall lights. "Pack those up. The ambulance is gone, eh? Go, look after the kid."

"Oh." I blinked at the sudden change in plans, but Rennie slung his satchel over his shoulder and collected a small pile of folders. They teetered in his arms, but before they fell he set a fast pace for the parking lot I'd helped mark out with reflective cones sometime around daybreak. "I'll— sure." I sighed.

So much for my non-date.

I flicked an annoyed glance over my shoulder toward the ambulance. Cole would know which hospital Paul would be taken to. The director's total lack of care factor bothered me, but I supposed we were all getting used to his weird sense of normality.

A check back at Rennie showed the dumpy little director already at the door to his hire car.

Something flashed there as Owen grabbed the light box and flicked off the power, leaving me blinded in an instantaneous blanket of impenetrable blackness. My phone was flat as a tack and utterly useless with nowhere to charge it all day, and I left my power bank in my hotel room. I counted a few steps into the void while my eyesight adjusted.

"Where are you?" I flapped at the spikey ground, dew already coating the prickly blades. My hand slapped a plastic cover. One of the folders Rennie carried lay on the ground just outside the filming area.

I grabbed it and tucked it against my clipboard, found my own bag, and turned to offer my apologies to Cole.

He stood alone a few steps away, watching the faint glow of the ambulance disappear up the highway. Thick arms were folded across his chest, his shoulders forming a defined line. The handsome Ranger's sex-appeal tripled in a moment but something far darker lay beneath his facade. An impenetrable, unyielding aura surrounded him.

I am a hopeless, terrible romantic for Texan men in white hats.

I'd spoken all of ten words to him and was

already half in love with the idea of the Texas Ranger. Pity I'd never get to fulfill that fantasy I probably shared with half of the crew.

"Cole, I'm sorry. I have to go to the hospital. If you can tell me which one to go to, that would be handy. And...where it is." A flat phone boded ill for directions but surely I'd be able to find a large medical building in Austin. That's where the ambulance would go, right? I couldn't recall any other city that close. Or maybe... I scrunched my eyes up in thought.

"Not a problem. I can help you out." Cole took a step in my direction. Even with my eyes closed I could *feel* his presence like a palpable thing.

I cracked an eye open in time to see him raise an open palm to Owen, who drove away...in the last remaining rental car. My lift back to civilization.

Thanks, dude.

My mouth twisted. Seriously, this had to be the worst organized work crew in the US. I scanned the slashed grass, but all the cars we arrived in were gone. The enormous, black truck that sat at the corner of the field was the only remaining vehicle. It had to be Cole's...which meant I was begging for a ride back to my hotel.

At least I'll be able to find the hospital.

I glanced up at him guiltily, already uncomfortable with the thought of asking, but there was no other way. I opened my mouth, but he beat me to it.

"It's not a problem, Josie. Don't stress it," he said easily. "Mind if I hang out with you at the hospital? I could murder a coffee." His dark eyes held me pinned for a moment, and he reached out a hand to wrap around my elbow, squeezing gently. "Plus, I haven't been much help today so...I'd love to actually be useful."

A ripple of electricity jolted through my shoulder at the minor contact, and his eye darkened, matching the star studded blackness above us.

I swallowed hard. "You were pretty handy back there." I looked up at him as he walked alongside me across the field toward the black truck that looked bigger with every step.

How in the hell am I getting up into that?

The back of Cole's hand brushed mine. If it had been Owen or—*god forbid, Rennie,* I suppressed a sickened sense of dread at the thought—I would have balked at the contact. But Cole's touch warmed me where I hadn't known I'd been cold.

"So, coffee, hospital, then dinner? If anything's open. You did well back there, not panicking." Cole squeezed my elbow gently and dropped it to open his truck door.

I stared up at the metal beast as he stood back

leaving me enough space to climb in on my own. My heart thudded against my chest when I glanced up at him to find him watching me with those star-darkened eyes. The faintest smile teased the corners of his lips.

I couldn't keep him. I didn't live in the area. Hell, I was a North Carolina girl who moved to California for college, and stuck in the very much not lucrative side of the film industry. Texas was so far out of my ball park I may as well be in a whole new land.

Which triggered my romantic side again.

"Damnit," I murmured under my breath, grabbing what looked like a handle and hoisting myself up.

"Damn what?" Cole slipped into the driver's seat with a single step.

"That I had to climb up like a kid who still has her training wheels on," I grouched, but kept a smile fixed on my face.

He grinned back. "Gotta give yourself more credit than that. You've got it all over those boys. And the odd girl I saw today."

He watched me? Warmth burst in my belly, rising to the region of my heart. "You must have been so bored today." I changed subjects, unwilling to be the central focus of his topic. "You were a different man when Paul...when he—" My throat closed up.

Cole's fingers left the gear shift and wrapped around mine. "Girl, you're freezing." He flicked on the heat, balancing the wheel on his knee. "Is Paul—is he a friend of yours?"

He cast me a sideways glance as he pulled back onto the main road that led back to Austin. The truck bumped on the verge a few times as we left the field but he didn't let go.

"I've worked with the crew all season. I'm an intern," I explained. "I graduated a few months ago and needed some actual work to build my CV. So, here I am."

"You want to make reality TV programs on Texas Rangers?" His grin sent tiny zings along my skin.

I squeezed his hand where he still hadn't let me go, ignoring the goosebumps that rose along my arm in ripples and wondered if I was experiencing the phenomena alone. "No. I'd like to make..." My throat dried. "Um, I'd like to work for a few of the bigger family channels. Like the year round Christmas ones that always have a happy ending." Hell that sounded so stupid even in my own ears. Cole coughed and my chest jolted. "Oh, god. I meant happily ever after." My face burned. "Not that sort of channel. Not that there's anything wrong with that..." I tugged my hand free, or tried to, ducking my chin to hide when my hair didn't do the job for me. "And now I'm super embarrassed for having such childish life goals."

I expected him to laugh. Almost everyone else I knew had when I tried to pitch my career plan to family or the —ex—boyfriend.

He didn't. Cole's gaze flicked from the road to our joined hands, the faint smile, so unlike the fake one he donned all day, decorating his face in the truck cabin's filtered light. "That's a decent goal. Good to know there's still girls out there who value family. And a damn good Christmas tree." He let my faux pas slip.

I smiled, grateful. "And ugly sweaters," I piped up. Mark Darcy featured in more than one non-daydream.

"And ugly sweaters," he agreed. Cole's hand shifted slightly, unfolding around mine.

Disappointment hit me square in the chest, but he closed his hand around my fingers, readjusting his grip to stroke his thumb over the back of my hand.

The tops of my breasts tingled like he touched me there instead. The intimate gesture left me short of breath. I focused on the road, unable to look at him as my cheeks heated. The lights of Austin grew brighter beyond the horizon, but we were still a good way out.

I frowned. "How did the ambulance get here so fast?"

"Smart girl." Cole's voice was quiet. "They were at a service for a friend of mine. Another Ranger. He worked hard all his life, and helped a lot of people. Spent a lot of time with the paramedics, making sure he worked the best way around them, too. Vince," he added to my enquiring look. "The official service was last week. I went to that, spoke to his wife, paid my respects. Some of the local service personnel held their own celebration of his life today."

And he missed the occasion that clearly meant so much to him for something as insane as Rennie's film.

"I'm so sorry you didn't get to go."

"I would have been working anyway. My unit—my old unit—deals with border control. Narcotics coming or going out, people trafficking. Some stolen goods and poaching, but it's mainly drugs and people."

"Did you always want to be a Ranger?" I twisted in my seat, leaving my hand in his, but I suddenly wanted to face him, to see what his face told me while he talked.

He pressed his foot down a little harder, and kept his eyes on the road. "Probably not much different from the girl who wants to film love stories and have Christmas all year round," he murmured.

Cole Vance could be a dangerous man to a girl who gave her heart so freely. He listened to what I said, and more importantly, he *remembered*. Not only was he handsome as hell with an infectious grin, but he also had a heart I could crave if I let myself.

Even if he was only a temporary fix for my lonely one.

CHAPTER THREE

COLE

I pulled into a spot a few blocks up from the hospital after dropping Josie at the door, promising coffee if she found her friend. Locking up, I prepared for a quick jog back. My heart clenched at the thought of her with the young kid, but she wasn't too much older than him as it was.

Just graduated...hell. A man nearly twenty years older than her should keep his hands off a girl that age. But the way she handled herself around her team spoke volumes of who she was, and with dreams like the ones she shared with me, she'd soar the moment she decided to put them into action. That same quiet determination and her spark of humor drew me to her in a distracting way I hadn't felt for far too long.

That she wasn't a local girl killed me. She'd probably set up camp in New York or LA, and I'd never see her again. Suddenly, eleven remaining documentary episodes seemed far too short.

Still...my hand curled, the warmth of her hesitant touch burned into my palm. I wanted to take her out for dinner, learn every secret she didn't know she possessed. Hell, I was all too ready to talk to her until the sun rose, then take her home and find out just how soft she felt against me with no barriers between us.

She's fresh out of college. I shook my head as I jogged the three blocks back to the emergency department. I was out of line hitting on a girl like her, but no matter how many times I pushed the thought of her aside, she returned to the front of my mind.

One day, and a decade of career determination is ruined because of a pretty face.

Josie was so much more than just a pretty face. I hadn't heard her whine all day, certainly a boon in comparison to the bemoaning of the rest of the crew under director D's lackluster authority.

I sucked in a deep, fast breath and pounded the sidewalk with my boots in a hard beat that matched my heart. It was a quick run, but after standing around for so long, I needed it. A coffee shop on the opposite corner to the hospital provided me with black ambrosia, and the nurse manning the front desk gave me the directions I needed.

I wound my way through the hospital's interior to find Josie leaning against a coffee machine opposite a closed door. A pair of plain clothed police stood either side of the room she stared into like she could access it with laser vision. The detective's faces were bland, showing zero emotion. This was just another long night in the making for a pair of cops who had plenty of paperwork to tackle back at the station.

Their presence told me everything I needed to know about the situation, but for now, I'd keep that to myself.

I gave Josie a small wave, stacking the coffees and silently asked her to wait with my eyes. A little warning not to intervene just yet slipped into my gaze, and I approached the cops when she watched me cautiously.

A few minutes later, they opened the door for me. I smiled, waited for them to back off, and ushered Josie inside.

I slid my hand around her waist for the simple pleasure of pulling her into my chest, memorizing her shape. "Make it quick," I murmured into her hair, inhaling coconut and vanilla notes that left me heady on my feet. "This is breaking every rule there is for all of us."

She tilted her head back, staring straight into my eyes, and nodded. When she walked over to Paul's bed, checking him over, I nearly hit the deck.

The girl stared straight through me like she owned me. It took every inch of control to not haul her against me and kiss her senseless on the spot, because in that moment I had zero control. She wiped it from me.

A few minutes passed while she read the chart, checked that he was alive, and straightened his sheets. She patted his hand, murmuring soft words I couldn't hear. My heart clenched at the sight. I wanted her hands in mine, and the thought of her sitting with the kid because she already loved him...I swallowed hard. Maybe it was her romantic notions but—anything I promised myself about keeping my hands off her was an utter lie, and I knew it.

I wanted her, far more than just in my bed, though that definitely played a solid part in my fantasy land.

"Thank you," she whispered, still clutching an armload of folders and clipboards. Her bag hung on one shoulder.

Sliding my hand beneath the strap I tugged gently, surprised when she let me take it. That shock lasted all of a second as I worked out how heavy the damn thing was. She rolled a shoulder, offering a grateful smile and led me out of the room. I nodded to the pair of cops who resumed their silent penance for the night shift, though their presence hit me hard enough.

Tomorrow would get me more answers once tests came back on what had happened to Paul. Josie's words still hung in the front of my mind. First, I wanted to spend some time with her—real time—before I turned all Mister Texas Ranger and got on with the job at hand. Not that this was the job I was here for.

"Let me take some of that," I held out my hands.

Her fingers whitened on the folder, and after a

moment she shook her head. "Thank you. But that's enough." Josie clutched her clipboard and folder to her chest like a shield against the world.

Or against me.

My smile tightened and I widened the gap between us infinitesimally, though it killed me not to touch her when she was right there.

Calm the fuck down, Vance.

"No problem." I shouldered the satchel, then broke every rule I set myself, sliding my hand across her lower back.

She swallowed but didn't move away, staring straight ahead, though the death grip she administered to the plastic folder eased up a little. "Did you want to try for a snack or, um—"

"Dinner?" I passed over one of the coffees. "I got black and a latte because I didn't know what you drank."

"God. Thank you. Black, please. Is there sugar in this?"

"No." I frowned. "I'll find you some."

She waved me away. "I prefer it thick and tasty, thanks."

I grinned and kept my face blank as I sipped the milky coffee that stuck in my throat. "Sounds like it's something else we have in common."

She watched me over the rim of her take away

cup, her eyes sparkling for the first time in what felt like hours. "How's that going down, Ranger?"

I grinned. "You got some sass, girl."

"Is that a good thing?" She took a large sip of her coffee and closed her eyes. "I think I love you."

I swallowed back some smushy as fuck comment, relieved she didn't witness my struggle. "Already? Glad I haven't lost it," I murmured.

Josie peered at me through slitted eyes. "I'm not the only sassy one."

"Touche." I tilted my head to one side. "That sushi place I mentioned is still open. I ended up parked in front of it. Wanna try that?"

"Sure." She tilted her head back again as we left the hospital. A pair of sugary sweet dimples formed by the corners of her mouth.

"Damn, you're cute." The words slipped out before I could catch them. I sucked in a breath of sharp night air. "Sorry, I—"

"Haven't flirted in a very long time, have you, Cole?" She surveyed me through those sparkling eyes, her lashes heavy and lush looking.

I shook my head ruefully. "No. Far too long." I slipped my arm tighter around her, drawing her into my side.

Josie's waist curved beneath my fingers, dipping violently in then flaring out at her hips.

My breath shuddered. If I didn't stop, I'd end up with her naked a hell of a lot faster than I wanted, and Josie...I planned on enjoying every single moment with her that I stole, even the clothed bits.

"Cole, wait." She stopped and faced me, her folders and half-drunk coffee clutched between us as a barrier.

I dropped my hand and waited. She had to be taken. Boyfriend? Girlfriend? Not at all interested? She was right. It had been way too long. I was well out of practice.

Josie inhaled a breath far too big for her slim frame and held out until I thought she might burst. "Are you married?"

"No." I blinked. That was it? "No, I'm not. With anyone at all." *What the actual fuck.* "Are you?" I asked carefully.

I learned the hard way back in training that one person asking about a partner or spouse doesn't mean that they don't have one of their own waiting in the wings.

"No." She was quiet for a moment. "I'm not usually a casual girl, Cole. But I want to see..." She blushed the cutest damn shade of crimson that stained her cheeks and trailed down her throat into her shirt.

"Josie." I caught her chin between my fingers in

a firm, gentle grip. She stared at me and stopped breathing as I leaned a little closer. "I really want to get...dinner."

A shower of giggles burst from her. "Damnit, Cole." She slapped at me in a half-hearted gesture.

I laughed at the darkened sky, wrapping my arm around her shoulder. This time she didn't flinch at the touch or remain stoic or panicked. Her arm pressed into my side, and she nestled her head on my shoulder.

"That's my girl," I said into the top of her head as we walked, not stopping to consider how much this would damn well hurt when I had to let her go in a few weeks' time. "Where did you go to college?"

"UCLA."

"Damn California."

"It's a bit of a hike."

"And a good school, from what I've heard." I nudged her toward the sushi place, grabbing the door and holding it for her.

"It was a great school." Her eyes twinkled at me again.

"What?" A small dose of defensiveness hit me, along with her vanilla and coconut scent. I leaned in to brush my lips over the top of her head. "You smell delicious."

"You can't say things like that!" She shushed me, rapping her knuckles against my shoulder.

"'Course I can. Hungry?" I wanted to devour her on the spot. No girl had the right to be so damn gorgeous and edible at the same time.

"Starving." She rolled her eyes, giving me another heady dose of her sort of sass that suited her to perfection. "Come on."

"I still haven't had that coffee." I should have been yawning, but talking to Josie ate away the hours before midnight. Finally the chef kicked us out, bowing us to the door and locking it firmly while we stood there, cuddling like a pair of curfew breaking teens.

Josie stifled a giggle. "I think he might want to go home."

"I know the feeling." I wound my arms around her, pulling her into my chest and spoke to her hair. If I pressed my lips to her skin I'd be screwed. "So do I."

"Cole—" She hesitated, leaning into me, but didn't say anything more.

"If you expect me to say I just want to go to sleep with you...I'd be lying." I slipped my fingers through the pale ribbons of her hair, watching her silky locks curl around my fingers, how they slipped around my callouses. "And I'm not in the habit of lying."

"Oh." Josie lifted her gaze to meet mine. Her pink lips parted, sweet breath brushing my mouth in the slightest tease.

"Oh?" I watched her. Playing games wasn't my style, but the girl was a decent set of years younger than me, and I didn't want to use that to take advantage of her. "Would you like to come with me? It's just a basic apartment I keep in town, because I usually live a lot farther south, and I'm still in transition shifting units. But it's clean, if unused. Or I can take you back to wherever you're staying, and say goodnight at the door."

She considered me for a full moment, sucking her bottom lip between her teeth and popping it back, the tender skin a little darker and more swollen than before.

I wanted to know what her mouth felt like beneath mine after I spent the next half a dozen hours kissing her. "If you say no, I'm good, Josie. I'll never push you. Not on something like that."

"I know." She raised up onto her toes and brushed her lips against mine in the barest touch that evacuated every drop of blood from my body and sent it straight to my cock. She smiled, her head tilted back. "That's why I'm saying yes."

It took every inch of restraint in me not to haul her against my truck and have her right there on the street.

"Good." I whispered. "Now please get in before I do something in public that will haunt us both for years."

Giggling, she let me help her into the passenger side of my truck. I took the time to run my hands over her hips, tracing the outline of her tights beneath her skirt and back up her inner thighs a tiny bit. Just enough to tease the fuck out of her until I had the privacy for my own little discovery tour.

"Cole," she squeaked, swatting at my hands.

Her nails scored lightly at the back of my knuckles, and I bit back a groan of my own, slamming the door before we both took it too far. Austin was a decent size, but her crew wasn't, and they'd be known everywhere by the end of the month. Giving her a bad rep straight up wasn't my intention.

I drove back to my hotel room with my fingers laced tightly around hers on my knee. I'd never been the possessive sort of lover—more the type of man who wanted a best friend at his side daily, someone to come home to after a huge week to a girl who had her own life but chose to share it with me.

Josie took those needs and delved deep, until all I could think of was her in my life every waking moment. I left her folders in the back of my truck, and drew her into the elevator, hitting the fourth floor.

"How long do we have?" Josie fiddled with her shirt, staring up at me through her lashes. She popped one button free, then the next, exposing creamy skin and the gentle slope of the valley between her breasts

"Not long enough." I backed her against the side of the lift, running my hands over her arms. Pressing to her, I cradled her face between my palms. "You want me to stop any time, I promise you I will. But I need you to tell me if you're not okay with something."

"I'm okay with it." She rubbed her nose against mine, let me rest my forehead against hers.

"Too fast, Josie. You don't know what I'll ask of you yet." I gripped her skirt in both hands, crumpling the material as I considered ripping it from her right there. "You have no idea who I am."

"Will you hurt me?" The tip of her tongue swept across her bottom lip.

"No. I'll never hurt you, unless you ask me to in your bed." I winced at the promise we both knew I'd break eventually, but she seemed to get what I meant.

"See? That's how I know." The elevator door slid open, and Josie ducked out from my arms, walking along the corridor ahead of me. Her hips swayed and I followed the motion, mesmerized. "Which one is it?"

I ran my door card over the sensor, waited until it turned green. The little light changed and I grabbed her arm, swinging her back to me. "This one."

"Cole–" Shock speared her eyes wide as I pulled her inside the darkened room.

The door barely shut before I pressed her against it, covering her mouth with mine in a hard kiss that left her panting and my cock aching.

"I waited all damn night to do that," I rasped.

My voice refused to work as I caught her cheeks in my hands, kissing her again until her soft lips opened for me. Groaning against her mouth, I slid my tongue along hers, dancing and sucking its length until she was a moaning, steaming hot little mess in my arms.

"Tell me you're still sure," I cradled her against me, offering her a gentle caress after demanding so much in our first kiss. Jesus, she tasted of new experiences and black coffee and innocence. "Tell me what you want, Josie," I whispered.

When she didn't respond, I kissed my way along her throat to nibble at the crook of her shoulder until she whimpered, writhing against me. Slim fingers tangled in my hair, urging my mouth back to hers. Josie kissed like a fucking wet dream, all hot lips, slick tongue and sweet as sugar. I groaned, lifting her up onto my hips. Her skirt bunched around curved thighs. Winding her legs around my waist, she kissed me, sliding her body against mine until I wanted to rip a hole in her tights and fuck her there in the entry way.

Her eyes glowed when she broke the kiss, both of us breathing ragged, shallow breaths.

"I want to not have to wait any longer to feel you inside me," she whispered, holding my gaze while my heart slammed to a stop at her words.

Gripping her round, full ass tight, I squeezed until she cried out. Knowing I'd leave marks on her, I held on and walked us into the bedroom, not bothering to kick the door shut.

CHAPTER FOUR

JOSIE

Cole deposited me on his bed without turning on any lights. "Tell me if you're attached to any of your clothes," he murmured, tugging at my top.

"I have to get to work in the morning," I

reminded him. I let him pull my shirt over my head, giggling as his knuckles grazed my ribs. "Stop that."

"You're ticklish?" A dark grin lit his voice.

"Oh, you have no idea."

My hands twisted behind my back, already working on my bra clasp when he launched at me, all light fingertips hitting my most sensitive spots on instinct. I writhed and yipped beneath his assault, twisting to get away from him but Cole was everywhere.

His thigh pressed between mine, skin to skin but I didn't have the breath to ask. I mounted my own attack, digging into his ribs, sliding my fingers along the soles of his feet, but nothing seemed to work.

"It's not fair," I fell back to the bed, panting. "You're not sensitive anywhere."

"You just haven't found the right places yet." Cole braced his body over mine, both of us devoid of clothing, and lowered his mouth to mine.

I sighed as his weight settled over me, his tongue gliding along mine, his kisses deep and slow, reigniting the need to feel him fill me.

"What places are those— *ohhh*." His fingers traced over the front of my tights, swirling in gentle, light patterns that sparked every nerve ending as he rubbed my around clit, his path aided by the slick that coated my skin.

"You remind me of the naughty librarian theory," he murmured. "All neat and tidy and proper. Then underneath...you're like my private playground, all spread out for me."

I whimpered as his fingers trailed over my breasts, twirling his fingers around my nipples until they stood out, beaded tight and more sensitive than almost any other part of me. "Cole—"

"Shh, sweet girl. Let me tease you, work you up for a bit. Rest back there," he cooed, already running his fingers over the stiff peaks of my nipples.

Alternating pinches with gentle tugs, he sent a myriad of pleasurable sparks running beneath my skin, each centered either on his touch or between my legs. I knew I'd be dripping when he finally touched me there again, and the thought tore another needy moan from my lips.

Cole kissed me, matching the strokes of his tongue to the swirls his fingers made over my nipples and my pussy, keeping his touch light in the promised tease. There was no way I'd be able to come the way he touched me. All I could do was let him drive me into a frenzy.

I gripped his shoulders, digging my nails into his skin and leaving small indentations the more he let the tease run on. His thick cock pressed into my thigh but he kept himself lifted away from my pussy, like he knew the moment we touched there was nothing that could stop our building momentum.

One hand pressed flat to my stomach, holding me down when I writhed at his touch. He circled my clit mercilessly, without contact where I needed it most. Heat gushed across the tops of my thighs and his dark smile grew. I knew he could smell my arousal. Hell, I could smell myself. Heat bloomed across my cheeks as I panted, fighting for his touch, needing it so damn bad I could barely think.

"I need you to touch me," I whispered, straining to close my thighs, to press them together and end this ruthless need for pressure before I screamed with the need.

He grazed his mouth over mine, slicing his tongue into my mouth in a brutal kiss that left me moaning and gasping, arching to him.

"That's it, Josie. Let me see you raw and wanting."

"Cole, please, *please*—"

"Please let you come? Please fuck you? Let me hear you say it." His hand teasing my nipples left my skin as he tangled his fingers in my hair to pull my head sharply back.

"Please, I need to feel you, skin to skin," I gasped. My nipples ached after his attention, my breasts tingling. "Please, Cole. Please."

When I thought he might kiss me, his head dipped lower. He licked the length of my throat, cupping his whole hand over my pussy. Grinding the heel of his hand over my clit, he pressed down hard until I was a writhing ball of sweat pinned beneath him as my orgasm hit me in full.

All his teasing touches culminated in a massive assault on my senses until I curled against his body, every inch of my shaking. My breaths came ragged, almost sobbing against him.

Cole gathered me in his arms, stroking my hair. "Shhh, sweet girl. Fuck, you're so beautiful. Let me do that to you again."

I whimpered at his words, unable to speak. I tilted my head back, begging for gentle kisses. He gave me those, too, taking my air and replacing it with head spins as my mind tried to play catch up on what he'd just done to me.

"I don't think I can move."

"That's a good thing." Cole stretched out on the bed, and drew me along his chest.

"What are you doing?" I clung to him, let him help me find balance.

"I'm holding a beautiful girl who I'm desperately trying not to rush." He stroked my hair in languid caresses, despite that it must have been mussed to hell.

"I get the feeling we're going to run out of night," I confessed, my cheeks burning at the admission.

I was never so forward with anyone. Cole...he made me comfortable. How I could not be comfortable when he did *that* to my body, I had no idea.

"Josie?"

"Yeah?"

"That sounded like an offer." His hands closed a little tighter on my back, his fingers digging into my skin, pressing me to his chest.

"I want to feel you over me. *All* of you," I suggested, raking my nails lightly over his chest.

"I don't want to hurt you." His eyes burned dark as he stared me down, unmoving.

"But I need you." I wiggled, swaying my hips side to side and curling my knee behind his calf, running my heel along the back of his thigh and pressing in. "Please?"

His Adam's apple worked as he trailed his searing gaze along my body. "Earn it."

"Huh?" I tried to lever myself up onto my elbows but there was no room, so I fell back onto the bed.

"Stay there." Cole's voice was hoarse as he watched me. "Touch yourself."

My breath stuttered. "I've never–"

"For me. Please." Cole slid a hand down my

stomach but instead of dipping his fingers between my thighs, he grasped his cock one handed and gave a rough jerk.

He flicked a foil packet out of his wallet and leaned back against the headboard, watching me through hooded eyes. His fingers tightened around his cock, and he gave it a few firm pumps.

I whimpered, unable to take my eyes off him. My hands slid over my breasts, playing with them the way he had, tweaking my nipples and moaning when the pressure was too much already. I pulled my tights off, peeling them to my knees as I traced lightly around my aching pussy the way he had. His eyes never left me, but each staining pump of his fist, each time his breath sped up gave me an indication he liked what he saw.

Scratch that. From the way his dark eyes hooded, his lips parting on a hard breath when I arched, stripped, playing with myself, he fucking loved it.

Which was what I wanted. The man had already given me the most powerful orgasm of my existence and made me ache...but we hadn't actually had sex yet. My body flushed hot, and liquid painted my thighs with need. I returned to my breasts, then dipped my fingers lower, tracing over my belly button and dipping between my legs.

Cole groaned. "Come here, sweet girl." His voice strained as he reached for the condom he left beside him.

"Wait," I whispered. His eyes narrowed. "No, not that. I just want to..." I couldn't force the words out of my mouth so instead of fighting with my own nature, I showed him.

Large, roughened fingers tangled in my hair as I slid my mouth over his hard length, taking his cock as far into my throat as I could on the first lick.

Cole groaned, pushing down a little, and I sank with his movement. "You are a fucking wet dream, you know that, girl?" He pinched at my nipples, soothing the sharp touch with gentle squeezes. I moaned, still sucking him. "Up here." He pulled me up, pressing the condom into my hands. "Will you?"

His cock popped out of my mouth, and I licked the tip one last time.

"Yes." I nodded, unrolling the condom with trembling hands.

"Josie." Cole's fingers tipped my head back until I had to look at him. "Are you okay? Do you want to stop?"

"No!" I almost shouted it at him. Cole's eyes widened and his hands opened. "No! I mean, I don't want to stop. You are— you're amazing. I don't want tonight to stop at all."

His larger, scarred hands covered mine, halting my progress. "I'm not pushing you into this?"

"Why would you be pushing me into this? I'm here because I want you as much as I think you want me."

"I do want you. So fucking bad." His mouth slammed over mine, wiping the world blank. His hands worked with mine over his cock until he strained, his hip jerking in my tentative grasp. "Let me."

His hands caught my ass, splitting me astride him. The tip of his cock pressed to the entrance of my pussy, the pressure a relief and a tease all at once. Cool air told me how wet I was, and I whimpered as he held my gaze, lowering me onto his cock an inch at a time.

I squeezed. My muscles fluttered around him the whole way down until I cried out, wrapping my arms around his neck for balance.

Cole gripped my hips tight. "Tell me I'm not hurting you, Josie?" He kissed my cheek, the corner of my mouth, my lips, all while impaling me on his thick cock.

The sensations were blissful and overwhelming. I moved, and he hit something deep inside me. A moan ripped free and I didn't care. "Please just fuck me."

"Yes, ma'am." Cole's hands closed on my waist, and he thrust up inside me.

I screamed softly, tipping my head back. My hair hung down my back, covering his hands while I ached for him, inside and out.

Moving with his body I found a rhythm that matched his, working my thighs until they burned with every rapid thrust. Letting him hold me up, I tilted my head back, pressing my hands to his shoulders as he assaulted my pussy in a way that branded the shape of him inside me.

I panted, biting back more screams as I ran my fingers over the hard planes of muscle that made up his chest and shoulders. Tracing my fingers over his body gave me as much pleasure, right up until he released my hips, cupped the back of my head, and kissed me senseless. Falling into him, I wrapped my arms around his shoulders, entwining our legs as he rolled me onto my back. A wildness entered his eyes that flushed me hot in a rush of desire, and drowned me in a searing river of pleasure and need.

I cried words I didn't remember as his thrusts drove home every inch of euphoria until his name filled the room in a raspy voice I recognized vaguely as my own. My legs wrapped around him, my hips convulsed, working for the last drops of pleasure from my own body.

Cole's hands wrapped tight around me as he set a punishing pace, pushing my body to its limits. Hard and rough, so different from the man I saw in him today, he swept me to the edge of rapture and took me plummeting with him over the side, my name dripping from his lips as he stared down at me like I was the only woman on his earth.

CHAPTER FIVE

COLE

Waking next to Josie was like seeing a sunrise for the first time. Her body curved into mine in a seamless fit, hot and searing until I knew I'd never want to wake up alone ever again. I traced the softened lines of her face with light fingertips, unwilling to wake her but unable to prevent myself from touching her.

Thick eyelashes fluttered against her cheeks. She stretched languorously, wrapping her arms around my neck when I leaned in to claim her mouth.

"Morning, Cole."

"Morning Josie." I kissed her again until her eyes were heavy with desire rather than sleep. My fingers curled into her hips as I pressed her back, letting my weight settle over her, and stopped.

"What?" Her eyes flashed open. She wiggled, but I'd set my mind to it. "What are you— please, I want to—"

"I know what you want." I laughed; it was the same damn thing I wanted, every day from here on out. "You have no idea how bad I want to fuck you right now so I can still feel your body where it pressed to me while you screamed. I want you to look at me like I've just had you every damn morning. That's why we're not."

"No?" Josie's brow dipped, and she pressed up for another kiss, an edge of desperation in her eyes I fucking loved. "Please?"

"No, you desperate, horny little thing. You'll have to wait."

"For what?" A wariness replaced the need in her eyes.

"For tonight." I watched her, let her come to her own conclusion.

"I can come back here tonight? We can— you want to—"

"Yes, I abso-fucking-lutely want to. Waking with you wrapped around me broke something. Or maybe I've wanted this and didn't know it until I found you. I have no idea how much time we have together. But if you want to share my bed each night, then I want to wake next to you."

Every day for the rest of my goddamn life.

But I didn't say that. I couldn't. In no universe did it sound sane to say that to a girl I met the day before under reasonably unusual circumstances.

Like the fact we have nothing—not a single, damned thing—in common apart from liking black coffee and sushi.

Had solid relationships been forged on less? I didn't know. What I did know was that years of being a street cop left me certain it took a tiny grain of sand to ruin a relationship with no other solid compass bearing.

Josie came from the sort of career based world I avoided. I lived in a shell bearing someone else's name half the time, one who didn't exist, cohabitating with criminals. I usually had the bonus pleasure of arresting them at the end of a long stint. Not a lifestyle made for romance, a family, or anything else steady.

"Are you sure you want me?" Josie stretched her arms above her head, oblivious to my inner turmoil. Her hips wiggled beneath me.

I gripped her tight, watching with satisfaction as her lips parted on the softest sigh. "I'm certain as hell. Now get up, cause we're both late already."

She stared at the window, and a long moment passed as she watched the sunlight filtering through dust motes of my apartment. "Oh. Oh! Shit."

I laughed, watching her scramble for her clothes and dreamed of a day I could wrap her in my shirt and make breakfast for us both with her wearing nothing else. Not that it would ever happen. Still, a man could dream.

For now, this was...kinda perfect.

I relished the idea of having her back here tonight, waiting to discover what other sorts of sounds she made with my head buried between her legs. I knew that fantasy would keep me going all day. But as dreams are wont to do, that one didn't work out the way I planned.

A new day, and a new location. This time instead of standing in the middle of a tundra, I perched on a rock like a shag, still grinning like a total dumbass, and tried not to eyefuck the pretty assistant who hasn't looked away from me for the past hour. Well, at least not visibly.

Josie gifted me a small smile as I was rearranged–again–and told to smile wider. *That's not happening.* My face felt like it'd split in two, and my retinas burned to ash many times over.

"Tell us why you joined the Texas Rangers," Director D suggested in a fake-happy-clappy voice that rattled my bones.

My mind went blank to a place where only crickets chirruped. Or in this case, water gurgled as it tumbled over smooth worn rocks and riverbed pebbles while the rest of the crew stared at me expectantly.

Including Josie.

Time to shine, sunshine.

"I started out as a kid who wanted to be a cop. What boy doesn't want to be the guy who saves the day? But it's more than that." I studied my hands. A tiny shard of laser light pointed right at the corner of my eyes reminded me to stare pensively into the lens directed my way, that damn red light on as always. "Heroes aren't born. They don't want to be described that way, and they sure as hell don't like talking about it."

Director D winced, but I barreled on. Fuck it. He could edit me out later or use that annoying little *bleep*.

"Being a cop was both everything I expected and nothing like what I needed, but when I was twenty, a greenhorn in all respects, and a freshly trained rookie, I didn't know that. I saw things I never expected, and lost my faith in humanity a few dozen times. I managed to regain that, too. Being a cop gives you a street level view of what people are capable of on both sides of a shifting moral line. Not everything is clear cut, or as simple a choice as the laws I relied on, the ones I believe in. How cop shows make reality look. It took years of working petty crimes, walking streets and my fudging my first undercover job to look...elsewhere." I edited my words before I said *higher*; nothing was more offensive to the cops and their spouses who would probably barrage me in their living rooms for it if they even saw the clip.

"The Texas Rangers take a small percentage of law enforcement officers when there's a need or vacancies." Like a real small percentage, but I didn't want to say that either. "That dream percolated for a while. And just as I got comfortable," I snorted softly, knowing the cameras would pick it up anyway, "I had a call from a guy down south I knew from that sh– undercover job." *Bleep me, asswipe.* "Turns out it wasn't all fail and something good came out of it. They made their arrests, and I got a white hat." I spin that same hat in my hands, smiling. "The birth of a new Texas Ranger determined to save the world, and no idea how to go about it."

"Cut." The director's tone was a little more muted than usual. "Take a break. Fifteen minutes. Be back here."

"Sir." The word slipped out of my mouth from pure habit even though I knew he was talking to everyone else. I settled my hat on my head and rose, stretching.

"Not bad, Ranger." Josie sidled up to me, a sassy little smile curving those lips I knew just what to do with.

"If you say so." I started walking, not looking at her in the event I gave myself away.

She followed, her shorter steps fast and hard, like her tone. "Hey, ego boy. What the hell–"

I rounded my truck where I parked it behind one of the vans that constantly traveled with the crew, grabbed her wrist and pushed her against the passenger door to my truck. Her lips parted, those pretty eyes flaring right before I slammed my mouth over hers. Her soft sounds and the way she wriggled reminded me I couldn't take it any further. Before I bruised her soft lips, I drew back, letting out a shuddering breath.

"Sorry." I couldn't help the broad grin that spread over my face.

"You are, huh?" She pouted, looking up at me through thick lashes devoid of makeup because she didn't have any at mine to put on. We definitely needed a trip to her motel to pick up her things. All of them.

"Nope. Not even a little bit." I lean one arm over her head, making her look up at me. Her fingers toy with the buttons on my shirt, and my cock hardened just at the thought of being skin to skin with her again. "Where are you staying? Wherever it is, cancel it. Pick your stuff up after and I'll take you to my place." I press my mouth to the corner of hers, expecting a decent dose of her sass and maybe a chest slap at my offer.

I got none of that.

Josie hesitated, and it killed me.

"I rushed you. I'm sorry." I leaned away but her hands crinkled in my shirt, halting my retreat. I eased back and watched her warily.

"No, you didn't—okay, yes you did, but only a little bit." The words tumble out of her mouth. "I want to. I really, really want to, Cole. But we got together yesterday. In pretty extreme circumstances. I want to stay with you, and I will. But...I also want to keep my room. Just in case. Because a girl should have options." She whispered that last like she's afraid of what I'd say.

Or what I'll do.

I gripped her chin firmly but gently. "Who the hell have you been dating that makes you afraid to say no to a man?" I murmured, grazing my mouth over hers. "If you don't want to stay with me, Josie, don't. I'm here regardless. I want you, but I'll never force you. Not ever."

Josie's lips parted on a soft sigh, her cheeks flaring with color even as her shoulders relaxed.

"Perfect."

That isn't the word her pretty, kiss-bitten lips formed, and it wasn't in her voice. I frowned as her eyes widened at the intrusion. I spun around.

Director Dickface stood behind us, a petty as fuck smirk fixed in place. I stared into a lens, sickened at the little red light on above it. "Good job, Janie. There's the emotion I was missing from his pathetic little spiel earlier." He turned away as fast as he arrived, taking my illusions and his camera crew with him.

"He doesn't even know your name." My voice

hardened as I looked at her. "If it wasn't obvious I didn't want to be the sacrificial lamb before, it damn well should be now."

"Cole, I didn't—"

"Did you set that up?" I ran over the way she approached me just then, by the stream. Was she looking for extra shots then already? Mind, she had a mouth on her but damn if I didn't find her sass the best thing this side of Austin. *Had* found it the best thing. Now... "Jesus. Was that a full set up last night, you getting left behind, with no one to take you home? Cause I'd question that man's methods and yours if you want a rep like his." I skimmed my gaze over her tight body, all those curves that fit my hands just right.

"No, I swear. I didn't know he would do that."

"Didn't you? Because the more I think about what sort of a tasty treat you are, the more I realize it's the sort of thing he *would* do. Hell, I should have stuck to the advice Archer gave me."

"Who?" She tipped her head back, eyeing me curiously.

"No one you need to know about." I snapped my jaw shut hard enough that my teeth clacked.

Josie winced prettily. Damn it, everything was pretty about her.

"Yes, he's an asshole to work for." She met my

gaze head on and gave her hair a little flip. "And that wasn't okay. But—"

"But?" I laughed harshly. "There are no 'buts' in this case, Josie. Fuck, no wonder you look frightened in case I said no." I shook my head, taking my hat off to rake my fingers through my hair, and slammed the damn thing back on. "Glad you didn't want to come back with me, Miss Josie. Consider that invitation rescinded."

I strode away from her, a sweet dream splintering in a moment's rage and passion that tangled together so tightly I couldn't separate them. But it doesn't matter, because that's all Josie was.

A dream.

CHAPTER SIX

JOSIE

Breath lodged in my throat preventing me from breathing as Cole walked away. I was glad of its presence there, because while I was turning blue, I *wasn't* sobbing hysterically at his back and creating the kind of scene that Director D relished and recorded.

Instead, I watched Cole walk away in silence and willed myself not to cry. The one good thing that came out of this whole damn shoot, and my time with him was up. Even I wasn't naive enough to know there was no coming back from the way he looked at me then.

Like I was nothing.

Like I broke his heart.

Which was stupid, because we had a fun night. A long night, and I'd hoped for more this morning. More kisses, more touches. Time to explore his body the way he did mine.

That would never happen now, because I chose to work with the biggest asshole director on the west coast for a job reference I knew he wouldn't provide at the end. That was the stellar sort of man Director D was.

And I...was the only one kidding myself.

Like any personal brand of loser, I watched him stride away from me, clinging to a heartstring I could play a miniature violin on. That lasted a full minute until Belinda, the director's assistant, darted in to grab at his sleeve, pulling him down to her barely five feet height and spoke quickly into his ear.

I watched with no little twinge of the green eyed

monster as Cole dipped his head and listened to her courteously, like he had with me, while she shredded his shirt sleeve, twisting it into a knot and dancing on her toes.

My mouth opened, insults all too ready on the back of my tongue, but I managed to close it before anything nasty fell out.

Like my pride, or my ego.

Was that what I looked like that night, scared and bending over Paul, left behind because I made myself so small as to be invisible?

The lump in my throat dissolved in full as Cole straightened, tipping his hat. I knew without hearing him that he reassured her in that deep smooth voice, the one made for calming old ladies and reclaiming lost kitty cats out of trees.

Well, I was a kitty cat and I'd climb any damn structure if it meant Cole turned back and listened.

That breath, the one that stopped me turning blue seconds before withered as Cole nodded firmly, tucked his hands in his pockets and walked away without a single glance at me, Belinda, or anyone else.

I wasn't alone in watching Cole as he walked away. Half the crew had eyes on him. But only one spent the night with him, and I knew those were memories I'd treasure, because they were the only ones I was going to get.

I deflated, heading back to the set, our fifteen minutes well and truly up. Not that the director cared a whit. It wasn't like he needed any other footage today. He got what he wanted, as always.

When Cole took his spot back on the rock, looking all things pensive and heart broken and handsome, the innate protector and too damn perfect from that whitened smile that matched his hat to his too-broad shoulders. Even his badge was too damn shiny. He never looked my way, and he spoke too quietly for the cameras to really catch him.

But this time, everyone listened.

Everyone, except me.

I couldn't watch, finding my clipboard and writing copious notes I didn't need, and buried myself in my work.

I pottered around my hotel room for the sixth night alone and unable to sleep. The television had nothing on I wanted to watch. Even the single movie, a historical police drama I usually would have sunk my teeth into and geeked out happily on my own did nothing for me. Once I turned that off, I went back to my notes, but ended up little other than an unflattering–though apt–caricature of Director Doof.

Finally, I tried to sleep.

After an hour of yet again cataloging all the nicotine stains on the ceiling of my non-smoking room, I pushed up onto my elbows, my mind whirling in a constant marathon stuck on the same thought over and over no matter how much I ignored it, just like Cole had ignored me for the last week.

Paul's incident wasn't the only one.

My clock read just after nine. What were the chances that the Austin Hospital would let a non-relative in a second time? Wiggling my nose, I tracked down the address on my phone, taking note of the coffee shop nearby, and checked their opening hours.

My luck held. If my bribe of caffeine and cookies didn't work, I'd resort to some bullshit emotional plea.

Austin at night was prettier than during the day. From a girl who lived in random spots around the country and based out of LA for the past four years, that was saying something. But the city was tidy, with enough character to dazzle gently. I walked the clean sidewalk, my arms wrapped around myself.

My lone hoodie—a gray metal band affair I stole off a previous boyfriend with just enough fleece to keep me warm—let me snuggle in. The scent of the previous owner along with any remaining faint once-emotional attachment was long gone.

Grabbing a triple stack of coffees from the shop from a dozy looking teen who might have had sloth in his veins, I found the empty fire escape and took the stairs up to the room where I last saw Paul.

Peeking into the semi empty corridor, I slipped through the doorway and breathed. Not a nurse in sight in the direction of Paul's room. I cast a glance over my shoulder and muffled a scream with one of the takeaway coffees.

"Not as sneaky as you thought, huh?" The nurse, a hard-faced woman with deep lines around her mouth, smiled, transforming into a slightly crazy version of Florence Nightingale.

"Apparently not." I smiled weakly. "Coffee?"

"Who are you here to see?" She sighed and scooped the bottom coffee from my stack—not the one I Frenched in a desperate bid not to drop the lot. "Boyfriend?"

I snorted. "That ship sailed, and not for the one

here," I added. "Paul Harris. He was brought in last night." Was it only last night? I rubbed a hand over my face, cuddling my coffees, praying I wouldn't drop the black ambrosia all over the floor. I had a feeling this nurse would make me clean it up myself.

"Popular man," she muttered, eyeing me and sipped the coffee. "You're lucky it's just me tonight. There's a staff meeting on, and I'm missing the party."

"Doesn't sound like there's a party to be missed."

She winced. "Probably not. Alright. You know which room he's in?"

I nodded. "Thank you. I don't think he has anyone else locally."

"He doesn't have anyone else at all. We tried to find emergency numbers for him, but he doesn't have any. The police took their samples and left."

"That's strange." I shifted from foot to foot as my hands started to sear.

"Sometimes we get an odd one." She waved me away down the hall, turning her back to me and muttering something unsavory about Californians.

I grinned, heading toward Paul's room. The rest of the hospital ward seemed so quiet, but as visiting hours were probably long ended, I didn't object, slipping through the door to his room and staring at his prostrate form. My smile faded as I studied the collection of tubes and beeping machines hoarded around him like silent sentinels. Perhaps they were, keeping him alive, breath after breath.

Damnit, I should have asked her if he's woken up.

"He hasn't."

I whirled around at the deep voice that startled me out of my reverie and came face to face with my second surprise of the night. This one was a little more unwelcome. My pulse sped up in a way that Nurse Hardass never managed to achieve.

"Cole." I nibbled my bottom lip, staring up at him. His face was more closed off than ever. A hundred questions raced through my mind, but there's only one I knew would actually break the ice. "Coffee?"

His lips twitched as he liberated the one on top and took a healthy slug. "Nice. Bribing the staff?"

"Yeah. That one's mine," I whispered through dry lips.

"Nothing I haven't tasted before." His hard eyes bore through me with an intensity that must be a bonus in his line of work.

Director D would kill for a glare like that right down the barrel of the camera.

I managed not to say that out loud. Not that he was glaring at me, exactly. More looking right through me, baring me to his gaze like I just stripped for him. Shivering, I hid in my hoodie and raised the fresh coffee to my lips. The heated drink soothed my insides, and I rallied because fighting back against Cole's intensity–or being swept away by it–seemed like equally stupid and fun self-destructive fates all at once.

"What are you doing here?" I could sound human around the sexy Ranger who hated me. Awesome. Proud moment right there.

"Same thing as you." Cole leaned back against the wall I suspected he had leaned against the entire time I enacted my little covert mission to sneak into Paul's room.

"Yeah, but why?" I peered up at him. "We're nothing to you."

He frowned at me and stepped away from the wall, invading my space. "Is that what you think of me? A figurehead, or a poster boy with no heart?"

A muscle ticked in his jaw as I stared at him, cataloging all the perfect parts again. Easy, white smile. Strong jaw. Blazing blue eyes and blonde hair. Forearms and shoulders to die for. Or on. And a few extras beneath the clothing... My cheeks radiated heat as I backed up anyway despite my determination not to let him intimidate me and stopped when my knees hit the end of Paul's bed.

Cole searched my eyes, narrowing his when he read the flush crawling up my cheeks in a telltale sign of heightened awareness. "You do think that. Fuck, Josie," he growled, sweeping a large hand through his hair. My body tightened, knowing exactly what it felt like to have those hands on me. "I thought you of all people would get it."

"Get that you're a playboy?" Why am I sassing him now? *Why?*

Cole made an exasperated sound. "I should take you back to mine and give you the spanking you deserve."

My mouth dried. "You wouldn't do that."

The unyielding stare he fixed on me said he absolutely would.

The way my body reacts said I might enjoy it.

I shifted sideways, needing more air than what existed in the tension lingering between us. "Okay, so I was just going to sit here with Paul for a bit and maybe talk–"

"Cynthia?" A man dressed in a rumpled cream suit–*who wears those outside of Panama in the eighties?*–poked his head into the room, cutting me off.

Cole pivoted slowly, giving me room to move away from him. "Wrong room?"

"Must be." The man waved a bouquet of carnations in a sea of baby's breath and wandered off.

I scooted around the edge of the bed, heading for the lone seat beside Paul, and breathed.

A vice grip wrapped around my wrist, halting my escape. "We need to talk," Cole said in a low voice.

"Maybe after my visit?" I squeezed my eyes shut at the lie that hung between us, fragile and ready to shatter...something. Trust, maybe. If we had any of that left over after today. "I saw you with that girl today." I closed my eyes. "Ignore my mouth. It's not communicating with my brain."

His fingers flexed on my wrist, squeezing gently. "You have a pretty mouth, Josie. I like how it works just fine."

I raised my eyes to meet his. "I thought you'd still be mad."

"At the director for being such a dick?" he snorted. "He's not your fault or your problem, honey. But if you don't like me talking to other girls...you getting jealous on me?"

"In your dreams." I shoved at his chest. A little coffee spilled out of the top of the takeaway cup onto the plastic lid. I licked it up, knowing his eyes were on me and made a meal out of it.

Not the time or the place...

"I mean, it depends what you guys were talking about. If she was asking you to take her to dinner, I'm okay. If it's sushi...yeah, I'm jealous."

Cole laughed softly, balancing my cup on his and placing both on a small side table. "It wasn't sushi."

"So I shouldn't be jealous?" I fluttered my eyelashes at him.

"No, you little brat. You shouldn't be worried."

"Who said I was worried?"

"She told me there were two others affected like Paul on the last set." His smile disappeared, his gaze heavy.

"Two?" Disquiet settles in my stomach. "I only know about one."

"Damnit, Tosie. That information would have been handy last night."

"I told you."

"When?"

"When Paul was rolling on the ground, drowning in a pool of pink spit," I snapped back, then clapped a hand over my mouth. "I'm sorry." I spoke through my fingers.

"It's okay, honey. It's been...madness. Wanna tell me what happened?" Cole peeled my fingers away, gripping both of my hands firmly.

"Not really?" I wince as his gaze hardened again. "Stop that. It's like looking into a void and falling."

"Huh?"

Okay, so my romanticized notions would never be popular with this literal man. That was a fault I could live with.

If I was staying in the state.

If I had a job to keep me here.

If...

I tried to focus but Cole being so close made that a tough job. "I mean, we were at Yosemite. He was debunking a scientist's claim there were new minerals surfacing. Ruined the guy's reputation fairly efficiently over six weeks."

He winced. "That better not be an ongoing trend."

"Maybe. Marc, a summer intern, was on the crew. He was outgoing, flirted with everyone—"

"Even you?" Cole's voice held a sharp quality I enjoyed far too much.

"Now who's green?"

"Get on with it." He smirked, lacing his fingers through mine. His thumbs turned small circles around the center of my palms until tingles raced along my arms and spine.

"Yes, even me." I paused to let that sink in.

"He asked you out?" Cole squeezed my hands a little tighter.

My playboy Ranger had his fair share of insecurities. His interview with a lens this morning proved that, and those fears resurrected behind his eyes with every word. I kinda liked that there was something not so perfect about this poster boy. Maybe I liked that way too much.

"Anyway, after a night around a bonfire involving a lot of alcohol and other things..." I wasn't sure if I could mention drugs around a man who had a history tracking narcotics across the border. Okay, fine I read his file. But that was my job. Or at least, I told myself that. "He woke up the next day with a massive hangover. Half the crew was. We didn't get a lot done, and Director D spent the morning in his van, writing scripts and terrorizing his pet scientist. Just before lunch Marc dropped, just like Paul. Pink froth, shaking. All the things. He went to the hospital. I wasn't close to him, and we moved onto the next project with half of a new crew. Not everyone lasts around the director."

"I get why. You said he didn't try to film that day?"

I shrugged. "There wasn't much point. The crew for the most part really was that bad then."

He huffed a laugh and released his death grip on my fingers. "Fair enough. So no one knows anything about Paul, and he's the third. Makes epilepsy or any other usual history unlikely."

"He hasn't woken up?" I bit my lips.

"Don't do that." Cole brushed his fingers across my bottom lip, resting his thumb there. He watched as I flicked the tip of my tongue against the intrusion. "And you all don't know each other much."

"You'd think. Right?" I pulled my head away, unsure if this was a man I wanted to get back into bed with no matter how much both my heart and my body ached for him.

We both knew that's where this was headed from the way he studied my mouth, how his touch set my skin alight, firing nerves that left me flushing hot and cold simultaneously.

"Yes. Six weeks in close company usually forges relationships. Same with the party culture." Cole's attention withdrew from me as he looked over my head and frowned. "Was Paul like that?"

"A party kid?" I winced at the ageist remark tumbling from my lips. "I think he's about four years younger than me. And I don't know him apart from saying hi, getting his coffee order, and collecting his taxes form. The director picked him up somewhere between California and Texas."

"Nothing obvious then."

"No. Are you...going to take this on, find out what's happening?" I held my breath. Would that mean more than the double handful of filming weeks he signed on for?

Cole's expression closed. "This isn't something I can do, Josie. I'm not a cop. Not anymore."

"But you are a Ranger," I blurted. "Isn't that supposed to mean something?"

"Yeah, it means I look after the girls getting trafficked across the border. Broken women who have been abused and raped since they were children. It means I socialize with the men who ruin them, and bring drugs into the US while trying to work out how the hell I can forge an arrest. It means I share meals with those men and pretend I share their... values. It means you're way out of your depth with someone like me. I'm so far from fucking perfect it's not funny, yet I get shoved in front of a camera and told to smile like a dog on command." The words left him in a venomous rush.

He's as terrified of normality as I am.

"If you think you're scaring me off with that, you're not."

"Maybe you should be scared." His easy going facade was replaced with the smoldering sort of intensity that tore through me.

I nodded, catching up with my train of thought in the face of a six-foot four-inch beautiful man flesh distraction. "I get that you resent the time wasted here, but isn't this the sort of thing that people need to hear?"

"They can get that on the tourist website, Josie." Cole raked a hand through his hair. "I need to be out doing my damn job so this sort of stuff doesn't happen."

"But isn't this your job?" I insisted, knowing I should stop, knowing I needed to let it go. Who the hell was I to tell this man how to do his job? A who had seen a whole lot of bad things in his life, screwed up, fixed that and come back for more? "What if we're the ones who need you?"

"Speaking from experience? This is something the local cops handle best. The Rangers are an umbrella unit. We look at different parts of the crime, where it originates from, how to stop that at the source. Like a big world view," He added helpfully.

"You mean this is too small for you to handle." I raise my chin. "It's okay to say you're a snob, Cole."

He reared back, dropping his hands. "That's not what I meant."

"Yeah? Damn sure sounded like it." I folded my arms over my chest.

"I'm not equipped for this sort of investigation." He held one open hand in Paul's direction as if in supplication.

"But you do know how to do it." My tone came out way too sharp.

I let all my disappointment at myself, my fear and anger from today, the distractions earlier in the night that wouldn't settle take hold. Man, could I grab that anger horse and ride that bad pony right outta town.

"Yes. I know how to do it."

I blinked. "That's it?"

"That's it." Cole's shoulders straightened subtly, but I saw it.

"You're an asshole." I slapped his chest and found his fingers securing my wrist again before I could go back for more.

"Probably not a good idea to abuse a Texas Ranger, hell child."

I stopped, my chest bubbling with laughter that wouldn't come. "I don't think anyone's ever called me that before."

"Yeah? What do you usually get?" He wound me into him, settling his free hand on my lower back.

Air evacuated from the room. I was glad Paul got his own mask and tank. And that he was unconscious, for just a few more moments.

"Um, the usual. Pumpkin, cutie...bitch if I piss someone off," I mumbled.

"That happen often?"

"My mouth gets me in trouble."

"I can tell." His tone was light, but his mouth stayed in a firm line.

I knew that last comment would come back to bite my ass at some point. Cole Vance wasn't the sort of man to let things go easily, and I was the center point of his attention right now.

"You're trouble. Me, too. How are we supposed to work together? This is a mess," I muttered, watching his fingers curl around my wrist, his hand too large next to mine.

"It is." Cole's grip changed, his fingertips pulsing against my skin, but he didn't release me.

I stared up at him, unsure what he wanted.

Lie.

"I need–" I swallowed hard. "I need to be able to breathe."

Cole laughed softly. "Cute." His arms wrapped around me, hauling me against his chest as he lowered his head. "But it's not enough to deny this."

"Deny what?" I played dumb, wanting to cringe but owned my bullshit anyway. Why not? It's not like I had anything more to lose with this man. He'd already torn my pride apart, and after two days he owned my heart, too.

The corner of his mouth crooked, his breath brushing my lips. "This."

Cole's mouth grazed mine just as my heart rate sped up to the point of a painful roaring in my ears. I couldn't concentrate on anything but him. His tongue swept over my bottom lip, leaving me gasping, my lips parted to admit him entry. My heart pounded too hard, thrashing in my chest as I pressed my body to his. Those rough hands pulled me flush into him.

I let out a soft moan, sliding my hands along his chest, measuring the plane of muscle beneath with my palms, though nothing had changed since he kissed me last. He was still the resolute man full of heartstrings and hard won strength. Nothing about him screamed *gym buff*; the way his body was built came down to DNA and whatever he did during his days as a Fanger.

One hand slid down my back to cup my ass, and he ground against me. His erection pressed hard against my belly, reminding me I wasn't dreaming or imagining that he wanted this as much as I did.

The sound between my ears increased to a screaming level, or maybe that sound came from outside my head.

"The hell?" Cole broke the kiss roughly, raising his head and glared at the machines that went haywire behind us.

Paul jerked twice in his bed, then lay still.

The machines quietened.

"No," I whispered, my mouth open in abject horror. "That—

"*NURSE!*" Cole bellowed, the sound reverberating around me as anger rolled off him, mingling with my fear. Not letting me go he stalked to the doorway and roared down the corridor.

If the single nurse on duty hadn't known about the change in Paul's monitors before, she did now. Along with the rest of the ward. Or the whole hospital.

My hardass nurse bolted toward us, not sparing a glare as she slid into the room on both feet and dashed to the bed. A second later an older doctor followed her in.

"Get out," he snapped to Cole.

The tall Ranger obeyed, snatching both coffees from my hands. He dragged me out the door and along the hall. "Give them room."

My head whipped between him and the doorway crammed with nurses and white coats. "Did Paul just— just—"

Cole's eyes offered no platitudes as he tucked me into his side and folded his arms around me in a shield against the oncoming barrage of medical staff who flurried into Paul's room and didn't emerge for a long time.

When they entered the hallway, every head was down. All their shouting and clamoring dissipated into an uneasy silence seasoned with a touch of finality.

Cole turned blazing eyes on me, a muscle thrumming in his jaw. "Tell me about the third case."

CHAPTER SEVEN

COLE

Josie sat at the opposite end of my sofa, wrapped in her heavy metal band hoodie that looked at least four sizes too large for her tiny frame, and nibbled on the sashimi she refused not to get on the way back from the hospital. That last wasn't an option, or so she informed me. Our resident sushi chef chattered quietly to his wife as he made a fresh dish for her and closed up for the night.

Which was how I ended up with the girl I thought I'd never have in my apartment again back in my living space.

One week without her after just twenty-four hours together, and the absence was hell. Every inch of her normalcy show was a facade she threw over a girl whose hand trembled in mine the moment I touched her. But damn if she wasn't the bravest person I'd been around for a long time. Paul's sudden death–right in front of us no less–was a shock to me and I'd seen that shit happen for years.

Josie didn't have that hardened shell. While I didn't want to coddle her exactly, I did watch for signs of a crash as it all hit home, and I had a plan of distraction ready to go the moment those trembles got worse...or stopped, and she started thinking.

Because I was desperate to stop her from having to deal with that right now, knowing exactly how that first time hit home all too well, a reminder that our mortality inched closer by the second. Most people can ignore that truth, but those faced with it sometimes on a daily basis–even the doctors and medical staff who attended Paul's room seconds after we lost him–hurt. Josie would feel it, but I'd lessen that onset of devastation if I could.

Hell, the only reason we were able to walk away was that I claimed I was there looking for evidence on his case. The doctors were more than forth-coming then once I named Josie as my assistant. Our badass nurse blessedly backed our bullshit story. They'd found no evidence of anything in his scans that led them to believe his seizure was brought on by natural causes. His toxicology report...that was another story.

"Okay, so you are going to investigate Paul's death, or whatever." She picked at her sashimi with bamboo chopsticks.

I winced at her flat, matter of fact tone. "You're going to mangle that, you know," I said quietly, watching her and not touching my own food. She raised her eyebrows. *Touche, hell child.* "Yes. I'll do a small investigation. Not that I have jurisdiction, and everything I find–if anything–is being reported directly to the local cops handling the case. I'm not pulling rank or claiming glory, Josie. Just the right guy at the right time sort of situation.@

"Cool." She shrugged and dissected her sashimi pedantically. "So what's first?"

I pressed my lips into a hard line. If this was her way of coping, so be it, but I predicted a crash on the horizon. "What's first is I learn everything I can about what happened in the previous cases. You've told me about Marc. Now I need to know about the third."

She looked up at me blankly, a piece of salmon dangling from her chopsticks. "I don't know anything about anyone else, Cole. I told you what I know."

"So I need to have a talk with Belinda. The girl who mentioned a third, " I added helpfully.

"Guess you are." Her tone–even her gaze– vagued out.

I leaned forward and caught her fingers, rescuing her dinner. My watch chimed the hour. *Fuck.* The last time I checked it was midnight when we left the hospital after I ran through all Paul's information–or lack thereof–with his team. Her dinner might as well be breakfast at this point.

"Honey. Pretty hell girl." I tucked her hair behind her ears, cupping her face and forcing her gaze to lock with mine. "Talk to me."

She flinched. A whole body effort that upset the tray balanced on her knees. I caught that too, setting it aside and scooted closer.

"There's nothing to say."

"Bullshit." I squeezed her jaw gently with one hand, my grip still firm but not painful. "I'm up in your face because you haven't reacted to someone you cared about dying in front of you, and it worries me."

"I didn't know him." Her flat tone was back.

"But you visited him. Twice that I know about. How many other people from your crew can claim that?" She said nothing though I gave her room to speak. "Josie. How many?"

"I don't know."

"Just you," I whispered. "That means either you cared about the guy, or—"

"I'm just a really lonely girl with no friends at work and figured I'd go and see the sick guy. Because if it happens to me, then maybe, *maybe* someone will come to see me, too. And now he's..." Her eyes filled with tears and every emotion she'd been pushing back seemed to slam into her at full force.

The crash came as I expected, if not in the exact form. Most witnesses I dealt with over the years cried hard to start, sob even, with the sort of panic that came on in a short lived version of immediate grief.

Josie's tears were the silent, constant sort that went on and on while she stared at me, her gaze brightening from that vague pit of nothingness back to conscious thought.

I held an arm out and she ducked under it, wrapping her arms around herself, her tears wetting my shirt. I tried to hold her but that damn sweater got in the way. "Can we get this off? It was built for a footballer and I can't even find you under this thing."

She hiccupped a soft giggle that warmed me from the inside out. "Give me a sec."

Josie disappeared into a ball and the black hoodie landed on my lap as she reappeared and curled into my side. "Better?"

Seeing you process the shit you should never have had to see if it wasn't for me?

I swallowed, grabbing the hoodie and tossing it on a recliner I bought but never used. The television was never used much either and I was rarely home long enough to make my home or anything in it look lived in.

The joys of working undercover. I still wasn't sure if that would be my purpose in Archer's unit, or if I'd end up working on my own caseload, either alone or with a partner.

Unlike every other Texas Ranger unit, Archer ran his ship under a slightly different structure. Considering the shit they faced together recently—heard first hand from Bear when I caught the drug trade on his southern patch of land—it was more than an honor to be asked into a unit that ran more as a family than anything else.

If I survived this stint with the production crew.

Not what I signed on for.

"Where'd you go?" Josie called me back.

I pressed my lips to the top of her head, breathing her in. "Just thinking, pretty thing. About my new job. I hadn't really started when I got pushed sideways into this. I'm glad I met you," I caught her chin, tipping her head back for a whole lot of eye contact I needed hard right then. "But the rest of the primping and forced scenes and...everything else... that I could do without," I finished carefully.

Josie's red-rimmed eyes held knowledge of things I wished she never had to witness. "Glad I met you, too."

"Why'd you take the job? With the director, I mean." I pulled her onto my lap, needing her closer. Maybe she wasn't the only one processing. "You know my story. Time for a little show and tell."

Josie sank into my embrace, and my heart thundered the entire time in my chest hard enough I was sure she must have been able to hear it from where her cheek pressed to my shoulder.

"I...it's hard, getting work," she started so softly I had to concentrate to hear her. "They don't tell you that at college. We're all gung ho, all promises of glitz and glamor and big name productions. But the reality is that even if you're good at what you do and understand the industry, it is tough. Sometimes it's who you know. Other times it's right time, right place." She lifted a shoulder and let it fall. "Sometimes it's good luck. I think the director was like that. I applied for the Yosemite job and I got it. Along with a brand new crew, except for his assistant. Your friend, Belinda."

I frowned. "I thought you were his assistant?"

"I'm the assistant to the director. She's his PA." She waved a hand. "Don't ask. Basically she kisses his ass more than I do and doesn't have to run coffees. I'm good with it," she goes on when I wince. "Honestly, it's fine. I get away from everyone for a few minutes. I get to breathe."

"Then this happens."

"Then this happens." She bit her lip and leaned back to hold my gaze. "I don't know what else I can tell you, but feel free to pick my brain. I'm good for it."

"It's okay, hell child. I'll figure it out." I leaned down and pressed my lips to the top of her nose as she stared at me in surprise.

"What was that for?"

"Because you're too damn cute for either my good or yours." Time to put that misdirection plan into place. I eased back, cupping her cheeks. "First, I want you to eat."

She shot me an irritated glance. "You too, then."

I stared down at my own full plate, having forgotten it entirely. "Deal."

We ate in silence until she bratted out on me and showed me her clean plate, making a meal of cleaning her chopsticks with her tongue.

If that's where we're at...

I finished mine, got her a glass of white wine and a beer for myself, and crooked a finger. "Come here."

She frowned. "I am here."

A laugh bubbled in my chest. "So literal." I leaned back, drawing her with me and threw the television on, not caring what program followed. "Like this." I wrapped my arms around her, resting her head on my chest. "Perfect."

She shivered, still tense against my body. "Don't you want to–"

"Didn't you hear what I said before?" I tucked a strand of hair behind her ear, conscious of the tightness growing across my own shoulders. Stiff, but not in the place I wanted to be. Well, not entirely. "I'm not the sort of man you should be with."

"What, because you're not *perfect*?" She air quoted me.

Sassy thing. "Because I'm never home and I can't do...this...ever. Apart from now. Like a little segue in my life that allows me to have you." I tapped her nose, but she didn't smile.

"My life doesn't stop either."

"So it's perfect, then."

She nipped at my fingers. "Smart ass."

"Brat."

Josie lay still on me for a full fifteen seconds. Her hands slid south first, and her body undulated gently against mine.

I let my head tip back and laughed. "You really are a horny little thing, aren't you? I promised a spanking," I warned, not in the least playful.

Josie smiled at me, a sassy as fuck grin that lit her entire face. "I know."

I groaned. "What the hell have I gotten myself into with you?"

"So much more than you knew." She wiggled her hips again.

My palm slammed down on her ass, and she let out a muffled cry into my chest. When she lifted her head, her eyes were damp.

"That fucking hurt, Cole." She swallowed, but her eyes never left mine.

Pink tendrils worked their way across her cheeks, and her lips parted on a soft breath between us. Not a single tear escaped, and though I knew the tears were real, I also knew something else.

"You liked it."

She nodded, a tiny admission, and held her breath.

I reached down to caress the same spot I spanked hard enough to leave my palm stinging. She moved a little as I massaged her, letting her rub her body against mine. My cock strained against my jeans, but my needs weren't what I focused on right then. Soft sounds tore from her lips, her eyes unfocussed.

Fuck me if that's not the prettiest sight I've ever laid eyes on.

Josie moaned a little louder, though I doubted she registered the cries that ripped me up from the inside out. I squeezed her ass again, and slapped her butt in the same place as before. A squeeze, and a spank. I went back to my massage.

Squeeze, *spank*.

Keeping my movements light, I drew her higher on my body, dragging her along me.

"You're hard," she whispered, grinding shame-lessly against me.

"I want you," I growled, pushing her hair back from her face, needing to see her eyes.

"Then why are we playing?" Her hands trembled on my chest, and I knew she was close.

Because if I fuck you again, I'll give you more than a good time, hell child.

Unable to form the words, I placed my other hand on her hip, holding her against my cock, rigid and straining. Then, I pushed down.

Her legs stiffened, sliding apart as she bore down on me. The sweetest little sound left her lips as she came hard. Short nails dug into my chest, her upper body arching a little before she collapsed on my chest with a soft breath.

I held her tight, promising myself I'd keep it clean from here on in. "You okay, Josie?"

"Jesus, Cole." She rested her forehead on my chest, her shoulders still heaving. "That was...what? A prelude to something tonight?" Her brow crinkled as she looked up at me with confusion written across her pretty gaze.

"That's because we're not fucking tonight," I said firmly. "No, you horny little thing. Tonight I want to spend the night making out with you and fully intend to fall asleep clothed and horrifically aroused for the hell of it."

She glared at me. "There's something wrong with you."

"Many things." I agreed with her wisdom.

"What about what I want?" Her inner brat, who was never far from the surface I was fast learning, came out to play.

"We'll get there, you little demon."

She pouted and placed her hands on my chest, peering at me through her lashes. "What if I'm all damp and need to be...clean?"

I grinned at the implication she was dirty. A filthy little mind, maybe. Throwing a thumb over my shoulder I kept my expression carefully blank. "Shower's that way."

"Asshole."

I spanked her lightly and she moaned outright. *Fuck,* it was a bad idea bringing her back here. Or a brilliant one. I hadn't decided yet. "That's your last one for a week if you keep this up," I warned her.

Josie grumbled under her breath while managing to slither up my body. That was a pretty feat in itself to watch. "Kiss?" she asked hopefully, tipping her chin up.

My gaze zeroed in on those pillowy, blush pink lips that parted to display the tip of her tongue wetting her bottom lip.

"You get what you asked for." I fisted her hair, and rolled her, grinding my body into hers. Our lips blended together as I kissed the shit out of her until my body ached, and I sweated through my shirt with need. Her hands worked their way under my shirt, seeking skin, and satisfaction. That's as far as I let her go, pulling her free and pinning her hands over her head as the sun rose, reminding me how short our time together was.

Then I kissed her some more.

CHAPTER EIGHT

JOSIE

I spent every night with Cole at his place for the next two weeks. Talking endlessly, though we didn't seem to have time for that during the day, kissing when we weren't. But despite a raunchy start to our Texan fling, after that night at the hospital he never let us go any further, no matter how many stops I pulled out.

Cole had determination, I'd give him that. But the way he stopped us, pulling tight on those reins of control he never released...it was like he was afraid of how fast our short time together was coming up. We were several weeks into a twelve week projected filming schedule that got shorter by the day. Now down to an adjusted timeline of ten weeks I could count off every one of those remaining weeks in my head.

Neither of us got much sleep, spending nights wrapped around each other, and I sure as hell didn't care that my eyes were hanging out of my head most days if I knew we had a few hours together waiting for us at the end of a long filming day.

On set, not a word was said about Paul. Not a single official announcement, or comment. After two days, I asked the director if he had a contact for funeral arrangements, but that ended in a threat of terminated employment.

Hating that I needed the money too much to not keep the job, I shut my mouth during work hours. Once I was with Cole in private, I got to cut loose, and I wasn't the only one.

And on day thirty-one of filming, what I knew he expected to happen hit us full force. Or rather, me.

"I need your bank account details if you want to get paid," I said to Jack Huston, trying to rein in my frustration at the man's avoidance.

What started as a simple check through paperwork released a field full of rampaging drama llamas. And my corralling skills were crappy.

"Can't you just issue me a check? I used to get those, easy to cash wherever," Jack whined at me.

Why did the crew have to behave like six year olds whenever anything to do with personal responsibility came up? *Why*?

That's right, because Director Indecent took them on without bothering with important stuff like you know, a contract, tax documents or bank account details. And when I wanted to give a month's pay out and figured I didn't have all the things I needed, I might as well have offered to pull teeth on a snarky gator.

"Would you like to be paid this month, Jacky boy? Because right now I'm seeing a bouncing check with a DIC signature on it." I swallowed my exasperation and tried to smile.

Fail.

Jack sniggered behind his hand at the acronym I gave our fearsome leader weeks back. Director In Charge, aka the DIC. Petty, but it fit the man and it fitted the general ambience.

"What's the problem?" The director sauntered over and walked right between us.

I lowered my clipboard, and clicked the top of my pen to showcase my exasperation. "I may as well not be here." I clicked the top of my pen several times in rapid succession for emphasis.

"Just trying to get my cheque and all," Jack weaseled his way into the other man's company, both of them standing with their backs to me.

"Fine." I muttered, seeing red. Backing up a few paces, I whirled around and ran straight into a brick wall wearing a pristine white shirt.

"Ow."

"Hey." Cole took a step back and leaned down to check my face. "Are you okay?"

"Am I bleeding?" I held out my palm to check. "You should watch that thing. It's a weapon."

Cole's laugh boomed around the set where we were parked on the edge of a random road. I had no idea what the artistic direction behind that stellar choice was, but I no longer questioned anything, aiming to simply survive this crew and already seeking future work in my few spare moments between the crew job and kissing Cole.

Priorities.

Hell, I'd even made an inquiry to a Texas based studio.

"You'll be fine." Cole patted my head in a condescending way.

My irritation skyrocketed. "Don't do that," I grumped.

"Wanna earn yourself another spanking?" His voice lowered, but not enough for my liking.

Torn between slapping him for ousting me of my fetish in public and bratting out just to prove a point, I went for middle ground and slapped my clipboard against his chest.

"I'm going on a coffee run. Do *not* ask me for anything." The current coffee stand was literally a folding table with an array of thermoses laid out with tags I wrote on earlier in the day. By now they were likely all stone cold, but I needed a breather.

"Done, hell child."

I glared at him. "Don't get your hopes up, Ranger boy. That spanking wasn't even that good."

"You came." His tone was smug and I would have slapped his face if the conversation behind me hadn't fallen silent right then.

Mortified, I tipped my head back and held Cole's eyes. *Give as good as you get.* "I've got a battery operated friend who has as much talent as you do, playboy."

Man, was he going to go to town over that one if

the glare he returned to meet mine head on held any promises.

Cole stepped forward, his eyes glittering. "Keep it up, hell girl. I'll find new ways to edge you with every inch of your clothes on...and mine."

My mouth dropped open. "You complete, utter as—"

A soft thud followed by swearing cut me off. I turned on my heel to find Jack on the ground, not a half dozen feet from where I stood, his body shaking and spittle foaming lightly at his mouth.

"Move, Josie." Cole's calm command got my feet going before the rest of me caught up.

He pushed by me, dropping to his knees in the dirt in a repeat of that first night while I hovered behind him. Cries went up around us, but I doubted he heard those or any of the whispers that circled the gathered crew.

Cole called for an ambulance, the only one of us really doing *anything* other than rubbernecking, while the director retreated not so discreetly, heading for his trailer, a string of unfavorable mutters and expletives following him.

One of the camera crew, David, edged closer. "Look at him work."

I nodded, unable to tear my eyes from Cole. "He's effective, that's for sure." A glance sideways tipped my world on its axis for a second. "Wait, are you filming this? What the fuck? Have some respect," I snapped as the first faint echoes of a siren reached us.

Cole glanced over his shoulder, checking me with a frown and sending an exasperated look at David who grinned sheepishly and lowered the camera.

"Delete that footage now," I muttered under my breath.

"No, don't. I'll take it as evidence." Cole rose as the ambulance pulled in.

He waved the paramedics over, dirt clinging to his knees as he spoke quietly to them. Even at a distance his silhouette was impressive, how he handled the pressure, the stresses.

"The man said to keep rolling." The camera was back on David's shoulder, the little red light on.

"No he did not," I hissed back, but the paramedics arrived, shooing us back.

"I'll need that." Cole held out his hand for the small mobile camera on David's shoulder.

"It's happening again." I turned accusing eyes on Cole, my burst of anger unreasonable, but I had nowhere else to put it. "I thought with you here it would all stop. You said you'd look into it."

"I am looking into it." Cole looked undisturbed

by my irrational hissy fit, calling another techie over and asking for the footage.

"You got it." The man disappeared with the device and returned a few breaths later with a flash drive Cole pocketed after writing his initials on the side.

"Why is it still happening?" I groused, unwilling to put an end to my fight just yet.

"Come here." Cole wrapped an arm around me, apparently not caring a whit that there were dozens of people milling about, all goggle eyed and whispering as he added fodder to the rumor mill. By tomorrow morning there would be several versions of the same rumor about us, and every one of them would be right.

Heedless of the glare I gave him, Cole folded me into his chest and held on as the shakes started in my hands and worked throughout my entire body. When the tremors finally stopped, he tipped my head back, kissed me in full view of everyone, and led me to his truck.

Jack lived, for now.

I leaned my head back on Cole's sofa, my eyes dropping shut. I wanted them to stay that way and block out every single thing that happened today. The whole affair was a clusterfuck of epic proportions and growing, starting with my hoodie. His house, his clothes, or that's how it seemed to go. My black sweater currently resided by the front door, outcast when I admitted it belonged to a former boyfriend.

Then I was presented with what was apparently more acceptable wear. The Ranger's branded hoodie in navy and white smelled like Cole, which meant that when he held me, I was wrapped up in him twice over. But that was a singular highlight of my shitty week.

Texas was no longer my favorite place. I wanted one Ranger to myself, and all the drama could rampage off somewhere else. I was so lost in my head I didn't register Cole's words until he repeated them a few times, taping my nose to draw my attention.

"Felix Shortman. Your predecessor." Cole held out his phone with a photo of a lean man with a ragged looking dark beard that covered a thin mouth and deep, close set eyes. "This is our third case."

"Of what?" I got the impression Cole knew a whole lot of something he wasn't sharing. Even though I had nothing to do with Paul or his investigation, it shit me that he didn't share when I'd given him...everything. Every single thing he asked for, and this was the first time he gave me anything. I tried not to lean forward like a too eager beaver, but in the end I couldn't help myself, snatching the phone from his hands and studying the photo.

"I don't know him." I handed back the phone, disappointed.

"You've never heard his name before? Seen the picture?" he prodded when I shook my head twice.

"Who was he?" Apart from the man's place I filled. Wait. Did that mean–

Cole nodded, reading the unspoken question in my eyes. "Yeah. I'm sorry, Josie."

Shit. He only used my name when it was important. I learned that fairly fast. At work, he was stiff and formal, hating the process and the lack of privacy. When it was just us, I was hell child, honey, or girl. Never pumpkin, thank God. But on the occasion he needed me to listen and not earn that first nickname to the nth degree, he used my name.

"Shit," I whispered, the implications falling over me like a thick blanket I couldn't worm my way out from underneath. "What about– about–"

Cole pressed his lips together and said nothing.

Somehow that was worse than him admitting that three people, young men, died working with the director. Recently. And that was just the ones we knew about.

"What if there are more?" I whispered, staring at Cole, but not really seeing him.

The vision of Paul flailing and jerking in the hospital bed was overlaid in my mind's eye by the first attack. Marc, his life bubbling away at the mouth. His arms trembling with the force of the seizure. But he seemed so healthy. So did Paul. Not that all syndromes and health issues were visible, but still...

My mind drifted to the bonfire with Marc. Belinda, singing her heart out to a stick she swore was a microphone the next day. Drinking around the fire. Marc, using the logs we pulled up as seats as a balance beam. Then—

Nothing.

I blinked, but nothing else was there. I remembered waking up the next day, as hung over as anyone. But I'd only had a few glasses of wine that Belinda shared with me when I hadn't brought along anything of my own. It wasn't even a consideration it would be a dry trip. It just never occurred to me to bring alcohol and recreational drugs on a work trip.

I was that green.

The pieces slowly dropped into place. I refocused on Cole. "Is this how it feels when it all comes together for you? Like this great revelation, then a sickening feeling because it is what it is?"

"What did you figure out, Josie?" Cole's voice was heavy, weighted with a secret I was about to tell him that he already knew.

That he knew already. Cole figured it out. That was the secret he kept.

And he used my name.

I nibbled my bottom lip. "Why didn't you tell me?"

"About?" He raised both eyebrows, prompting me.

"About the drugs, Cole," I said, exasperated. "Marc. He used them at the bonfire night in Yosemite. Paul. He socialized and went out the night before. Do drugs usually take that long to hit your system? And what about– about–" I scrounged for the third name and came up blank.

"Felix? Yes, he used drugs as well, though his habit was a little harder than the others. I need to find the source."

"Where are they coming from? I frowned. "Is this related to the sorts of drugs here, in Texas? The ones you stopped coming across the border?"

He hesitated for a beat. "Yes. But the effects of this sort of designer drug is...odd. Like it's meant to do one thing but affects the body in another way later on. Has anyone offered you anything?" He kept his tone light, but I could almost hear him thinking.

He wasn't alone in that.

"No. I don't do drugs. I tried pot once, in college. Hated the smell and spewed. That turned me off pretty much everything. I don't really drink much either." I shrugged. "As a student I never had the budget. As me now...I still don't have the budget but also I don't have the time. Usually I work my ass off after hours but I kinda figured the job out a bit better this time around and my time is taken up with...you."

Cole raised his eyebrows. "That was quite a speech."

"Damn right." I considered. With the extra brain space, my mind cranking over, a few extras fell into place. "Wait, is this why you haven't talked to me at work? Because you're what, undercover again?" I broke off and silence fell in his apartment. "Cole? Did you get approval or whatever to do this for the duration of the show?"

He held my gaze for a long moment then nodded once. "Is that what you think?"

"And that's why you weren't talking to me. I *knew* something was wrong. I knew it. But then..." I stared at the floor, the weight of his attention on me, then raised my head, everything clear as that freaking romantic looking stream we filmed near weeks ago. "Me. Us. Everyone. You don't know who, so you won't get close to anyone in case…"

Cole leaned back, spreading his thick arms across the back of the sofa. "It's the job. I needed to talk to everyone."

That was it. He didn't say anything else.

"You don't trust me."

"I didn't know you."

I swallowed that one, managed not to spit it back at him, and rose on unsteady feet. He held out a hand to help me but I waved him away. "I'm good."

"Josie."

"No."

"Hell child—"

"Fuck you," I shouted, whirling away and striding for the door. I grabbed my discarded hoodie, threw his to the floor, and walked out with my head held high.

Then I made it all the way around the block, knowing he didn't follow me, didn't even get up when I walked out of his door. I slid down the building onto the sidewalk, and cried.

CHAPTER NINE

COLE

Fuck. I never meant to hurt her that way. It was all too easy to fall back into the *I don't give a fuck about anyone else* undercover persona, usually the easy going guy, though this was the first time I used my own home and my real name. Which made it twice as easy to justify letting her go when she ran from me.

By the time I hauled my Ranger ass down the stairs, my heart hurt like hell and I could barely breathe.

"Josie?" I yelled into a silent street with no traffic whatsoever.

Yanking my phone from my pocket I sent off a quick message, and kept it in my palm, waiting for her response.

> Cole: I'm sorry, Josie.

> Cole: I didn't mean to hurt you. Let me know you're safe if you won't come back.

I waited, flipping my phone over in my hand but she never responded. No three little dots, no sassy remarks telling me where to go. Blowing out a breath I paced in a circle, feeling less than useless and walked halfway around the block in each direction, checking my messages constantly.

Nothing.

I squeezed my eyes shut. I could follow her to the accommodation where she hadn't stayed for a few weeks and make a scene, or I could let her have her privacy and talk to her in the morning.

Squeezing my phone, I debated in silence on the

sidewalk. Would she want me to find her, or did she need time?

> Cole: Do you want me to come to you? I'm sorry, Josie. I was an asshole.

I got no response, no matter how many times I checked, or how long I waited.

My heart fractured as I turned away from the street and headed inside. Tomorrow. I would get to the next filming site damn early and talk to her tomorrow. Heading back up to my apartment, I kept an eye out in case she never left the building at all.

The little hellion was probably sitting on my sofa, ready to rip me a new one. But my living space was empty, just like the cavity in my chest.

I absently collected the hoodie I leant her, burying my face in it for a moment, then dragged my sorry ass to bed. The next hours were spent trying not to replay the conversation in my head a thousand times, over and over, and concocting new ways to apologize in the hope she'd take me back.

Because I loved her. It was the only reason I held back from her, knowing it was stupid, knowing I should have taken every moment possible and used its maximum potential. Smart, sassy, stunning... *perfectly imperfect.* I knew some others wouldn't like a mouth like hers, but I fucking loved that she thought for herself.

I only hoped that same connection was strong enough in her that maybe I hadn't broken both our hearts.

I lay on my back, staring at the darkened ceiling, and prayed she would let me talk to her and apologize on my knees the next time I saw her.

I'm sorry, Josie.

The set was a muted scene as the sun rose above the horizon. The crew hadn't moved location from the roadside, which made it easy to find them coming in early. And though the rest of Texas was still asleep, this crew hauled their asses out of bed and tried to get the job they were set done despite the hindrance of their director.

Before I pulled up I knew she wasn't there.

"Have you seen Josie?" I asked the cameraman who shot the extra footage I knew he hadn't deleted yesterday. "I need to talk to her."

The man—David, maybe?—stared at me, a wide smile breaking out across his face. "Lover's quarrel, eh?" He laughed loud enough to draw the attention of the entire crew.

Fuck me. But it will have to do.

"I'm looking for Josie," I called, turning in a tight circle.

Blank faces stared back at me.

"She came home fairly upset last night." A soft, feminine voice spoke to my back.

I swiveled on my heel to face Belinda. Short hair bobbed around her face in puffy bangs, her bright eyes and bushy tail not cute or sweet, only annoying today. She flirted with me each time I needed information and though it was frustrating, I didn't say anything, knowing I needed to work beside her for several weeks.

With the *come fuck me* eyes she fluttered my way at daybreak, I wish I had.

I cleared my throat. "I'm looking for Josie," I repeated like a robot version of myself. "Has she arrived?"

Belinda shook her head, a small smile playing on the corners of her lips. "I haven't seen her since she came in crying last night. But I can help you look for her, if you like?" She held out a hand and gave a little wiggle.

Christ. Not now.

A second thought followed hot on the heels of the first.

"She can't drive."

Belinda looked immeasurably happy with that. "No. No, she can't."

"And if everyone is here, how is she getting in?" I glued my tongue to the roof of my mouth at her reddening face in response to my question before I said something unsuitable to get us both fired. When she said nothing after a long moment I reversed that decision and sighed. "Forget it. I'll find her." *And apologize my ass off. Beg her to come back with me. Get down on one knee.*

That last thought wasn't half as terrifying as it might have been weeks back.

I dug in my pocket for my keys and flung them in the air, catching them one handed as I strode toward my truck.

"You won't find her there."

I closed my eyes, and let my mouth run. "I don't have time for games and bullshit. There's a job out there that needs doing, and you're stopping me from getting to it with every tactic you use to slow production down."

"Is that what I'm doing?" she called sweetly to my back.

Fuck. I didn't have time for this. Not answering her I made it to my truck, pulling the passenger door open.

"You might want to try the hospital, man." The

dude with the camera constantly attached to his shoulder jogged up to me. "Belinda's right. She had a drink last night, bawled everywhere and ran off. You did a number on her." He frowned at me like I was a statue fallen from its pedestal and spiderwebbed with cracks that weren't there before.

"We fought," I said shortly, refusing to go any farther into it than that with a man who hadn't spoken to me before yesterday.

"She visited the other guy. Maybe she's there this time."

"Maybe." I revved the engine and pulled the door shut, winding down the window. "Thanks."

"Good luck." He watched me drive away, his reflection wavering in the wing mirror, though the damn little red light on his camera never flickered.

Nurse Badass—I didn't ask her name this time around either—pointed me in the right direction, shaking her head. "I haven't seen her, though the pair of you are adept at getting into places you shouldn't."

"I should have brought you coffee." Not that she was remiss in ripping me a new one. Right now I deserved it. "If you see her before I do, can you please ask her to call me?"

"Have a falling out, did you? Let me tell you something, Mister Texas Ranger. That girl likes you. She might even love you. But she isn't from here, and she won't stay unless you give her a good reason to put down roots."

I nodded, grateful for the unsolicited advice but needed to get moving. My feet took off for me as I waved my gratitude over my shoulder. "Appreciate it."

"Four-oh-nine. That's the room you need." She mumbled something unfriendly to my back.

She could curse at me all she wanted. What I needed was to find a pretty girl with a sassy attitude and a quick mind. But when I found Jack's room, the man lay alone in his bed, connected to a dozen machines. Thumping my fist lightly against the door frame, I headed back to the desk where my nurse waited.

"Not there?" She gave me a sympathetic look. "Try her usual places. Then wait. If she doesn't come to you, you'll know."

"Unless she wants me to go to her." I raked my hand through my hair. "This isn't the part I'm good at."

"Then you want to get good at it, Ranger. The

world can fall apart, but that girl needs to be able to count on you." Her face hardened as she watched me.

I didn't need a second opinion to know she was right.

"Ma'am."

I headed back to the street level and drove out to the shitty, cheap ass motel the Director put the crew up in. Jammed between a Walmart and a burger joint, the place looked industrial, and smelled worse.

"Josie?" I knocked on her door with my knuckles, and waited. The same sense of emptiness I got the night before assailed me. I raised my hand to knock again, and my phone vibrated in my pocket. "Vance."

"You called me." Brodie's soft voice filtered through the morning light as the occupants in the motel began to stir.

I had, the night before, then a message needing information, and assurance I wasn't overstepping my bounds. "I did. Is there anything you can help me with?" I'd spoken with the man once before during an undercover operation that involved his father.

"Right now...not a lot. It's an opiate. If it's in their system, the drug makes the person drowsy.

Mixed with alcohol they forget more of the previous day. But later, the effect hits the body and it goes haywire. No one can tell me why, but I've seen it before."

"Where?" I held my breath.

"In my father's house. He was distributing it lightly. Called it *el sueño*. The Dream."

One they might not wake up from. *Fucking awesome.* Josie's Californian was rubbing off on me.

Brodie's accent thickened. "But he pulled it back when he realized people died too fast. Not good for repeat customers."

"Yeah, what drug dealer has a conscience, huh?" I shook my head. "Any information on how to tackle the OD cases? The hospital might want a chat."

"No idea." He breathed out heavily into the speaker.

"What?" I frowned.

"Like I said. I know nothing about what it's cut with that makes it dirty, and from what you're saying with pink foam...it's a different incarnation from what I've seen." Brodie fell silent.

"Got it. Thank you," I said, raising my hand to rap on Josie's door again.

"You're welcome. Let me know when you're back down my way."

"You're not in Texas at the moment?" I knew he

did a lot of undercover work and spent more time in Mexico than he did at home.

"Yeah, there's always some bullshit to tidy up down here. That shit grows like fungus if I turn my back." The son of the largest cartel boss south of the border laughed darkly. "They've asked me more than once if I want to take up the vacant position."

"What, you don't see yourself as a mob boss?" I teased.

"Not on the cards. Not for me, princess," he bantered back. "But I've got a stripper pole here with your name on it."

"Hold that for me and I'll get back to you." I paused. "How does that work with your girl? Heading out all the time."

"Staying apart? We manage, man. It's part of the job. She understands, and she has her own life. When we're together... it's magic."

Magic, not perfect. Maybe I was aiming too high with that bar. I knew he and the stolen girl he brought back over the border were tight, and he adored her. But they made it work. Maybe –if I hadn't fucked up too badly with Josie, and I could find her before she turned tail and fled to California– we could give it a try.

A real try.

"Thank you. On all fronts. I'll send you through

anything we get on this new drug. If you have a chance to stop it...do it. We've lost two straight up. I don't want to make it a third."

"On it." He hung up.

I flipped my phone in my hand, watching Josie's door and called out once more. "Josie?"

When silence was the only thing that greeted me, I pulled a pocket knife out that had a few custom, handmade attachments I added to it years ago and jimmied the lock. Her door popped open seconds later. I was glad my phone was in my hand, unlocked, because I needed it.

Josie lay on her bed, on her back. White foam decorated the corners of her mouth, and no matter how hard I stared in a moment that drew out into an eternity, I swore her chest wasn't moving.

For a heartbeat, neither did mine.

CHAPTER TEN

COLE

I've never been so fucking frightened in all my life.

Watching Josie's chest unmoving broke me. My knees hit the industrial carpeted floor that was long overdue for replacement beside her bed as I leaned over her chest and pressed my ear against her heart.

A pair of too-slow thumps rewarded me with a breath of my own as I dialed for an ambulance. Josie's hands were too cold, her circulation slowing as I clung to her, rolling her onto her side and checked her breathing continued unobstructed.

"You're gonna be fine, hell child. Promise. We're gonna get you to the hospital and all fixed up."

Every word was bullshit. The doctors hadn't figured out how to help the people coming in, and when two thirds of the cases I knew of died, my heart bled with the pressure I put on it.

Hoping.

"Come on, Josie. I need you to wake up for me. Let me apologize for being an utter asshole last night. I spoke to Brodie this morning, and the boy slapped some sense into me. You remember I told you about him?" No response. Maybe I hadn't, so I stared fresh, winding my fingers through hers. "He's an undercover Ranger who brought home a girl..."

I kept talking after the paramedics arrived. Even when they put her in the ambulance and let the crazy man who wouldn't let her go climb in, too. Nurse badass ripped me a new one the moment she was settled in her ward, after triage.

I didn't care. All I wanted was for my little hellion to wake up and do it herself.

Just wake up.

Josie's machines beeped while I napped with my head on her bed, unwilling to leave the room. I counted out the days it took to lose Paul, recounted the story I knew about Marc, the bonfire night guy.

Jack down the hall–he was still beeping at the same rate as Josie. So there was hope. I raised my head, my eyes bleary and dry as I brushed hair back from her temples, and wiped a tiny drop of saliva from the corner of her mouth.

"It's okay, pretty girl. We'll fix this. Somehow. I'm so sorry I pushed you away. Hang out for me, yeah?"

"Keep on talking." Nurse Badass–Tabitha, when I finally asked–flurried around me, checking stats and Josie's pulse on the other side of the bed.

"Does it help?" I frowned at her.

She shrugged. "Who knows. But it makes you feel better, and you're the one here running the rumor mill, so go gossip at her."

I huffed a laugh. "Love it, Tabby Cat."

She frowned at me and let out a little hiss, flicking black enamel claws our way as she backed from the room.

Damn, that woman made this hospital come alive.

The thought sank deep as I turned my attention back to Josie. Her lips were set in a small smile and as I leaned forward, her eyes flickered open.

"You gonna fight her on everything?" she whispered, reaching a shaky hand for me.

"Every single thing," I promised, grabbing her hand and kissing her knuckles, her palm, her wrist. "Anything, just keep on staying awake for me, hell child. Tabitha!" I yelled in the same breath.

The nurse barreled into the room, and came to a stop when Josie offered her a watery smile. "Good to see you're awake. Let me take some measurements and get the doctor for you." She wrote new stars from the machines on the back of her hand, and gave me a sugary sweet smile as she swept out of the room. "Told you talking to her was good for you both."

Josie laughed, a dry, raspy sound in any case.

I let her have it.

Two days later I sat in the interview room on the ground floor at Ranger HQ in Austin. Josie curled on the plain seat next to me, her legs tucked beneath her. Though pale, she came back to her usual self with a vengeance. With a little help from the medical team, the local cops, and Brodie, we found the pair of culprits who were arrested a few hours ago.

Plus, Jack also woke up and gave me the handful of information I needed in order to close the case off at the local precinct.

Josie wanted closure, and before they were hauled off to County, I made the call. It wasn't like I could say no to the girl who cried with me when I admitted I thought I lost her.

Tabitha helped, poking her head in to remind Josie I'd sat there all day with her, talking to myself like a loon and praying.

Apparently, that put me in Josie's good books, because my girl hadn't fought with me a whit over my behavior the night before, and for that I was more grateful than I could say. Her future, and mine, were still undecided as I sat across the table from two people who caused multiple deaths and a hell of a lot of side served suffering amongst their crew.

The director and Belinda.

The first looked bored. The latter was still flirting with me, even handcuffed to the table.

"Why?" Josie picked at the threads on the hoodie she wore.

My hoodie, the one I brought to the hospital for her. She giggled then until her sides hurt, clinging to me, and turned her face up for the sweetest kind of kiss a guy can get.

We managed to turn it into something pornographic within seconds.

And Josie wore the hoodie.

"Because we needed a test market."

"Money."

Belinda's answer and the director's mashed together all at once until I couldn't work out who was saying what.

"That's cute. Maybe you can share a jail cell and combine notes. Then you might have a strategy to get people killed *and* achieve your goals." Josie snarked. She closed her eyes and rested her head on my shoulder. "Was it fun, watching them die?"

I winced internally, knowing how this one would play out. But Josie was determined to see the worse humanity had to offer. I was just there as moral support.

"Do you think they deserved better deaths?" Belinda answered when the director didn't.

Josie balked. I pulled my arm tight around her, but she shrugged part of the way out of my hold. My girl wasn't the only one with a sense of stubbornness.

"Better deaths?" Her voice rose. "What sort of a psycho are you?"

I squeezed her firmly in my hold, half clinging to her to prevent the girl from launching over the table and getting herself locked up on someone else's behalf. "We can go." I signaled the cop at the door waiting to take the director and his assistant away.

"No. I want to hear her answer." Josie sank into her seat and folded her arms.

"Hell child," I murmured. "We can talk it over at home."

"Asshole," she shot back, not an iota of playfulness in her eyes or tone. "I need this."

I sighed, raking my hands through my hair and let her have this one, too. "Okay." I could pick up the pieces later.

Belinda beamed, like her fifteen minutes of fame had come at last. "You're so fucking innocent," she said with a smile. "We needed a testing ground to ensure the drug worked. The first batch didn't. I had the chemist make up a fresh batch with a few tweaks. You might have seen him once. Older man, white suit. He came to see your...friend."

Her tone implied there was no friendship about it all but my back straightened as I nodded to the cop at the door who took notes.

Josie stared. "You gave me something different? In my wine?"

Fuck, Brodie mentioned mixing *el sueño* with

alcohol. But if Belinda was talking about something else, we might as well be back to the drawing board, or at least close to it.

Belinda's sugary sweet smile twisted into a smirk. "Thought it would be fun to see if a little underweight thing like you could deal with it. Remember much about that night?" She studied her nails and winked at me.

What the actual fuck.

My mouth ran dry as I put it together.

Josie hadn't forgiven me. She couldn't, because she *didn't fucking remember why she was in her damn room and mot mine.* I swallowed hard.

"That's enough." I nodded to the cop as Josie looked at me in confusion. "We need to talk. Upstairs. There's an office we can use."

"I'm not finished." Josie frowned at me.

"You will be in a minute. Byeee." Belinda waved, her farewell all singsong and fluffy and downright evil as I barreled Josie through the door and hit the call button for the elevator.

"What on earth is going on?" Josie rounded on me.

Her hands slapped my chest, her eyes full of fire despite that the doctors told me she'd be fairly out of it and not to push her for the first week at least. Before any other therapy or anything else was considered, though she didn't want anything. My job was simply to look after her, seeing as her father, her only remaining relative, wasn't in a fit state to travel.

I huffed a laugh and caught her face in my hands. Before I fessed up and she walked—again—I needed one thing from her. My mouth grazed hers in a chaste kiss, but she rose on her toes before I could take my next breath, sealing our lips together.

All coherent thought left my brain as I thrust my tongue into her mouth, kissing her wildly. My fingers dug into her scalp as I twisted my fists through her hair, and she pulled my shirt tight enough at the front I thought it might actually come off.

"Please," she begged softly as I broke the kiss, letting us both take long breaths, our hands still tangled around each other. "It's been so long."

A few weeks, sure, but it felt like an eternity. "Agreed. First, I need to talk to you." I found her hand and pressed the button to get us moving.

"We can talk here." She frowned at me. "Cole—"

The door opened and a man with rust-red hair and a matching beard with hard eyes wearing a white hat over the lot stared at us.

"Archer." I nodded. "Josie, this is my new boss. The reason I'm on your show—" I broke off.

The show folded after the director's arrest and the crew turned tail and fled back to California. The last woman standing was the one next to me.

"I'm his girlfriend." She held out her hand, and Archer shook it.

"Good to meet you, Josie." He turned to me. "And good job on the case. It went through as I expected."

I tried not to blink my surprise and fucked that up, too. "That was a test."

"Brodie kept an eye on you. You were never alone."

"Right." I wasn't sure if I should be furious or grateful. "We lost a man."

"That would have happened whether you were there or not. There's a cadre of bodies scattered across Mexico that haunt Brodie too, Ranger. Talk to him about how he deals with it, and struggles. He'll be honest with you. Got a formal event to get to." The stocky man grimaced. "Not my favorite part of the job. We're all there. Office's yours. See you early tomorrow." He tipped his hat to Josie who smiled and squeezed my hand.

I stared at my new boss. "Uh, thanks."

"Lovely to meet you." Josie towed me out of the elevator. The large office seemed too broad after the confining box that contained my deflated ego just fine. "This is nice." She ran her fingers along each vacant desk, reading the nameplates. "This one's yours."

"It's what now?" I spun to face her, breaking from my study of the room.

The last time I was here the place was filled with the rest of the team chattering and hurling general shit at each other while I headed into Archer's internal office set off to one side with a lockable door.

Now, in the empty space, none of it seemed quite real.

"What did you say?" I swallowed thickly.

"This one's got your name on it." Josie pointed to a triangular wooden name plate with *Cole Vance* engraved on a brass plaque.

"He got it made up," I said stupidly, staring at the mostly empty desk.

Mostly, as a screen, laptop, and trays occupied the top. A manilla folder sat to one side, a name I couldn't quite read scrawled on it. Archer made up the name plate, and set up my desk before I completed the assignment. The one I didn't know I was on in the first place, or at least part of it.

Paint the Texas Rangers in a good light and you'll be fine.

I assumed I needed to put my best foot forward presentation wise. He meant something different.

That handwritten name on the folder called to me. I reached for it, but Josie's voice stopped me.

"You wanted to talk."

"I did." I turned to face her, planting my ass on the corner of the desk and held out a hand. "A confession. I didn't realize the drug fucked with your memory, hell girl. Last night. We fought." I cleared my throat as she walked toward me, letting me fold her hand in mine. "I was an asshole. You walked away. Ran away, actually, and it took my dumbass far too long to claw my way out of my head and chase you. By then you were gone. If we hadn't fought, Belinda wouldn't have had a chance to drug you." My throat burned, and my eyes. Fuck it, I nearly lost her because of my ego and being in my head that night. "I'm sorry, Josie. It was bad, and I'm not telling it well. But you ran for a reason. I understand why, and I don't expect you to stay."

Josie stared at me, wide eyed. "That was quite a speech."

"You should hear me in full form." I cupped her cheek, savoring the feel of my palm pressed to her soft skin and grazed my thumb over her lips, enjoying the moment in case it was the last time she let me touch her. "Nothing's here to hold you to

Texas. I—" Hell, we never talked too much about families. "I get it if you want to leave."

"But?" she looked up at me expectantly, her eyes clear.

"But?" I stared at her. "Didn't you hear what I said? That I've been saying to you all along? I'm not fit to cohabitate with anyone, let alone a pretty Californian girl I've not right to claim as mi—"

Josie pushed up on her toes and tipped her head back. "I'm short, so meet me halfway or this won't work," she huffed.

"Are you sure?" I frowned at her. "I want you here, Josie. Believe me. But—"

"But nothing. Belinda asked me if I remembered. I never got to answer her." Josie's grin was all *cat got the cream*. "I remember every assholic moment of last night, every tear I shed when my heart broke again and again. And if you had lied to me just now I would have walked out the door and you wouldn't have heard from me ever again." She drew breath. "But you did, and here I am."

"That's quite a speech."

Her eyes narrowed. "Shut up and kiss me, Ranger."

EPILOGUE

JOSIE

"Four."

Cole's broad hand made for spankings connected with my bare ass, heating an already sore spot. "Thank me, you little hellion."

"Thank you, Cole," I sassed him all happy and singsong.

He growled and delivered a flurry of spanks in short order I struggled to keep count of. My Texas Ranger seemed intent on banging the sass out of me daily and I was more than happy to deliver him an extra helping the moment we were done.

A particularly hard slap to my ass cheeks left me moaning and dripping over his knee. So good I forgot to count. Or thank him.

Cole's spanks stopped. "What do you say, hell child?" he asked dangerously.

"Thank you," I whispered in my bliss-induced haze, settling my cheek—the one of my face, not my butt—against the comforter of the bed we shared.

He urged until I couldn't say no, sending for my things in storage from California to fill his house. Not that I had much, jumping straight from college to on the road crew style work.

Now, I was settled in Austin, with my Texas Ranger who had a spanking fetish that matched mine, and a job at a local Austin film studio. A small one that concentrated on Texas history, and showing what life was like on both sides of the borders—north and south—and how that influenced the populace. Including the ongoing Ranger's war against narcotics smuggled into the US. They even agreed to do a Christmas special.

It suited me and I got to peel plenty of information about Cole's investigations from him, even when he didn't realize he was doing it. Anything to fill the hole in my heart that still gaped at being drugged without consent, twice. Because bonfire night and no memories after a single glass of wine that never bothered me before.

I could have died twice and the shakes that ripped through me for days afterward, that feeling of *wrongness* sat with me week after week. My new therapist said it would fade.

I found a Texas Ranger who would help me through that phase and let me forget.

"Thank you, Cole," I repeated, sinking lower on the bed. My thighs relaxed over his knees, and the spanking ceased. "What?"

He laughed darkly. "Girl, if we keep going I'm gonna lose you, and I want you to feel every damn thing we do tonight."

"Oh." That sounded reasonable. "Okay."

"Fuck, I love your sass. And you. But this?" He hauled me up until I coiled boneless and naked and dripping with need on his fully clothed lap. "This is what I want to come home to. See my little brat happy with her...therapy."

After a solid bottle of wine one night with him I confessed my therapy theory. The next day, he took me up on it.

Now it was part of our routine. Sometimes light, others harder, depending on his mood, and mine.

We always, *always* made hard love afterward.

I still wasn't sure which part was my favorite.

Cole's fingers trailed between my breasts, pausing to tweak a nipple. I sighed, nuzzling into his shoulder and licked at the fabric between us.

"Get naked?" I suggested.

"Wait." His command gave me pause as his hand glided along my stomach, and between my legs. He played with my wetness, sliding his fingers through my slick folds and buried three fingers straight inside me.

I cried out, rocking forward. "Too much.'

"Not for you. Come for me." His mouth crooked up at the corners sinfully as I stared at him, my confusion evidently written across my face. He kissed the corner of my mouth. "Ride my hand, Josie. Come for me nice and hard."

I whimpered, my body already ignoring me and obeying him as I rocked and rose and fell over the thick, long fingers he positioned in the perfect place. My thighs ached as I pushed my body hard, undulating and moaning. Each breath came hard as the pressure built. My hands fell to his shoulders, holding tight for balance as I fucked his hand with abandon.

Just as my orgasm crested, he closed his hand hard around my pussy like a clamp. The heel dug against my clit, pinning the throbbing nub in place. His fingers flattened out as he gripped me, holding me still as I stopped riding him and took on the wave of pleasure instead.

I crashed into his chest, moaning and sobbing with the force of it all. He clasped my tight, his damp fingers tangling in my hair to hold me against him. I didn't care.

"I'm making you all sweaty," I whispered as he lifted me and placed me tenderly in the middle of the bed, rearranging me on my stomach just the way he wanted with my legs together.

A finger ran through the crack of my ass and he squeezed one warmed globe, delivering an extra spank.

I moaned and nuzzled into the blankets. "I like that."

"And I don't give a shit about getting...damp." Cole's clothes were off in record time or maybe I dozed in my blissed out state as his body pressed to mine.

"Good. Because I'm slippery from you," I

murmured into my arms crossed beneath my head, unable to do much of anything, except feel.

He seemed to love that he put me in that state, and so it worked.

Cole's cock rubbed down my crack, and he pushed against my pussy. My swollen skin parted easily to admit his entrance, and he filled me in one long, hard stroke that left us both breathless and moaning.

"I love you," I whispered, not really thinking about what I was saying at all.

"Yeah?" Cole stilled, kissing along my spine while I shivered, then settled his weight against me. His hands folded over my hips, roughened fingers digging into my skin. "Hold on to something, Jodie. This is going to be hard."

I nodded, completely ignoring him and clenched his cock with my pussy. "Can't wait."

"Sassy thing." He swore softly, working his hips in a slow rhythm that I was certain he designed to drive us both slowly mad.

"I thought you said hard?" I tipped my head back, begging him silently for a kiss.

His mouth closed over mine, our tongues tangling and sliding together in a slow, sensual kiss that left me gushing.

"You like that, huh?" His finger dug deeper into

my hips as he kept to his word, working us together wildly until we both shouted our pleasure to the world, uncaring who heard, as long as there was us.

Just us.

That's all who mattered.

THANK YOU
FOR READING

I hope you loved Cole and Josie's story. Please leave a review. If you haven't read through my Texas Rangers series,

Read Texan Devils and start with RANGER'S WISH in my favorite second chance romance ever with the perfect ending.

Love cowboys? Read RED HART RANCH.

ABOUT THE AUTHOR

USA Today Bestselling author Sofia Aves writes fast-paced police romances, sizzling military units, steamy cowboys with a Montana backdrop and the occasional cheeky god. Sofia writes kidlit for charity and has over one hundred and fifty publications across six not-so-super-secret pen names. As acquisitions editor for Evernight and Evernight Teen publishing she loves discovering new talent in romance and YA spaces, and is a mum of three crazies in a returned veteran household. Sofia has two overly large fur babies who think they're teacup puppies, a duck who prefers to eat from a dog bowl and two axolotls named after a dragon and a firebird.

Sofia lives near Brisbane, Australia, where she has her own alpaca park, Lorendel.

www.sofiaaves.com

Sign up to Sofia's newsletter and get a free Blue Blooded Brothers book.

Haven't read the Z Boy's prequel? Get it for free here:

A TABLE FOR TEN

Follow Sofia on

BookBub

Twitter

Instagram

Facebook

READ SOFIA'S SERIES

Blue Blooded Brothers

Collision

Politics & Paperwork

Blindsided

Sentinel

Mugshots & Candy Canes

Impact

Reckoning

Red Hart Ranch

Snow on the Range

Siren on the Range

Sundown on the Range

Spirit on the Range

Ash on the Range

Mistletoe on the Range (2025)

Forgotten Mountain Man

Texan Devils

Ranger's Wish

Ranger Bedevilled

Ranger's Passion

Ranger's Fury

Ranger's Wrath

Ranger's Storm

Snapdragons & Seductions

Summer with a Ranger

Merry with a Ranger

Beach Duty Collection

Playing to Win

Off Boarding

Vicious Slash

Zero Pointer

Off Stage Fling

Rippton Allstars

Crushing It

Glacial Force

Rippton Creatives

Study Games

Make Me, Break Me

Twisted Obsession

Spring Break with a Mafia Prince

A Royally Fake French Menage

Angel Shot

Jericho Chimeras

Puck Me Always

Puck My Heart

Puck me Sideways

Z Boys

King

Joker

Hearts

Ace

Mayhem & Mistletoe

Ruski

Fast Track to Love

Speed Trap

Klauss Brothers

Zander

Keegan

Gallo Empire *with Jade Marshall*

Splintered Vows

Fractured Vows

Fierce Vows

Savage Covenant

Rom Coms

She's A Hot Christmas Mess

Boats, Moats and Root Beer Floats

Writing Romantasy as
SOFIA SHELLEY

Dead Poets Sorority

Writing Reverse Harem Dark Romance as
DOVE PRIEST
Recurve Ridge

Kidlit writing as
JO SEYSENER
The OCD Elf
The OCD Elf's Great Reindeer Calamity
Greg and the Egg

writing YA as
JOSS PHOENIX
Alchem Academy
HIDE FROM US

Writing spicy paranormal romance as
RAVEN HUSH
Club Fray
Darkest Desires
Purge
Kidnapped By Claws
Ruin
Shadow Lords
Sinner's End
Heaven's Gate (2026)

Monster Brides

Phoenix's Eternal Flame

Kraken's Vow

Krampus' Christmas Bride

Silent Sentinels Duet

Reflections of Silence

Echoes in the Void

Monsters In New York

Feral Moon Rising

Dark Water Refuge